I0671428

Unsanctioned

Devilish #2

Charity Parkerson

Punk & Sissy Publications

Copyright

—Warning: This book is intended for readers over the age of 18. Some of my books contain allusions to past abuse and trauma.

Contents

Introduction

WOLVES AND VAMPIRES CAN'T be fated mates. That's just how it works... or so they thought.

As alpha of the northwest Were pack, Waylon is accustomed to a stoic life of duty. It's his job to guarantee his pack's safety and ensure they thrive. That duty doesn't include love. He's lived a long time, and now every Were he sees looks like a pup to him. That's not appealing in the least. Then a king's guard moved to town, and he's perfect in every way for Waylon, except one. He's a vampire.

Audor was born a Viking. That's who he'll always be at heart. When King Jonathan sent him to the north to watch over the small town of Wulfe, Audor gladly obeyed. After all, as his ancestors would say, it was fortunate to be favored. Unfortunately, he's never been as blessed in love. Until he met a massive wolf with sad eyes, and now Audor is twice as unlucky. Odin has forbidden vampire/Were pairings. This is a dream doomed to fail... or is it?

Unsanctioned is the second book in Charity Parkerson's Devilish series where vampires, Weres, demons, gods, and all manner of the supernatural live together beneath the noses of humankind. These books are best when read in order.

Chapter One

THE CRISP NIGHT AIR had more than a chill. It was downright freezing. Thankfully, Waylon's thick coat of fur protected him from the bitter cold. As always, he took one last run around his property, ensuring everything was secure for the night. The scent of a pack member filled his nostrils. His heart crawled into his throat. Randall's mate was pregnant. The only reason he would be headed Waylon's way would be for an emergency.

His front paws dug into the dirt as he shot forward, running at top speed toward the smell. He skidded to a stop, and Randall did the same when they came face to face.

Ashka is in labor.

Waylon heard the panic in Randall's mind. *Lead the way.*

They took off running toward Randall's house. Waylon fought the way his heart raced with fear. An unfortunate number of Were babies didn't survive birth. That was why their numbers stayed so low. Weres immediately healed after any sort of injury. Everything about birth was purposeful physical damage. While humans took that destruction and slowly healed after giving birth, Weres healed every step of the way, making labor take forever while killing the babies and sometimes the mother. Even though Weres were almost impossible to kill, giving birth was as traumatic as it came. Few wolves even risked it any longer, but—for some—the reward outweighed the risk.

An odd calm fell over Waylon as the house came into view. As the pack's alpha, he had to be the steady one. In this case, his calm came externally. He felt Ashka's peace. She wasn't in horrible pain or struggling. A smile tugged at Waylon's lips as he became human. She wasn't alone.

"Thank the Gods. Frost is here."

Randall nodded. "He showed up without being called right when I left to get you. Still, it's your right to be here."

Waylon slapped Randall's shoulder and squeezed. "Celeste sent us a healer for a reason."

Randall tried for a small smile, but his terror was thick. It nearly choked Waylon. They headed inside together. Heavy breathing could be heard the second they stepped through the door. The living room had been transformed into a makeshift hospital room. The sexy doctor Celeste had sent to their town was already positioned between Ashka's legs. Frost's mate, Gemini, sat nearby with his back turned out of respect, but was ready to jump in at a moment's notice.

"Hey, baby," Ashka panted out between breaths behind a mask she wore that looked like an oxygen mask from an air-plane.

Waylon smiled. It was as if she only saw her mate. Waylon took up position with Gemini. Frost didn't look away from his job, but he also didn't ignore the room full of terrified males.

"She's being given a large and steady dose of nitrous oxide, and I'm giving her doses of pain medicine at safe intervals. Her blood will burn through each shot quicker, but the less pain, the more re-laxed she'll be. That's important for the baby's safety."

"What about her safety?" Randall barked out, sounding more wolf than man.

"I'm fine," Ashka answered for him. "As long as I know our baby is okay, I can do this."

Waylon had been so focused on Frost's explanation, he didn't notice the tiny heartbeat sound beeping in the background. His throat swelled. He wanted this for the couple. They were such a small community. It wasn't uncommon for members to travel often, hoping to meet their mate. Randall had found Ashka while on a trip to New Orleans. It seemed she had been a bartender at the southeast pack leader's bar. The odds of meeting a fated mate under those circumstances were so slim, but Randall had done it. They deserved this blessing. Waylon silently prayed to any god listening while Ashka gritted her teeth through a large contraction.

"Okay. That's good. You're doing great." Frost was so calm. It was catching. "Here comes the part we talked about. When this next contraction hits, you'll push, but don't stop when the contraction ends. We're going to push until this baby pops out enough for me to do the rest."

Ashka didn't respond, but Waylon felt her determination. He also felt her slight panic as the pain built again. She knew the moment had come of no going back. Either they would survive, or they wouldn't. It was a hell of a thing to face. Yet she handled it like a warrior. A loud scream tore from Ashka, but she kept going. He swore she likely shattered her teeth with the way she clamped them. Randall was a mess, but trying to hide it. Gemini was poised to fight should anything happen, and the pack turned on Frost in their need to blame someone.

"That's it. You're doing great. Don't stop. I'm about to make that cut."

He felt Ashka's pain, but she didn't make a sound. All her focus was on pushing. Then she collapsed. Randall hovered over her, babbling nonstop and making no sense. Everyone held their breath. Waylon knew Ashka was fine. Just exhausted. He could hear her thoughts. It was the baby he couldn't feel. Frost's body blocked everything from view. Waylon could tell he was frantically working, but he couldn't tell what happened. Then he heard it. The tiny cry. Followed closely by Ashka's howl of relief. Her tears flowed freely as Frost stood. He passed the tiniest baby

Waylon had ever seen to Ashka. "Congratulations on your daughter."

Waylon swiped at his cheeks when he felt the moisture rolling down. He stood. "I am so humbled by your strength, and we are beyond blessed to have your daughter as part of this pack."

Ashka flashed him a tired-looking smile. "Thank you." Her eyes and nose were red. She looked beautiful. "I appreciate you lending your strength."

Waylon knew he hadn't done anything, but that was what being a pack meant. He was their leader. His presence mattered to them. That was why it was so important he never failed at this position.

"Rest. I'll come by when you're ready to have guests."

She nodded and went back to staring at the tiny bundle in her arms. Frost gave the couple instructions. Gemini patted his back. "I'll walk out with you and give them their privacy."

Waylon took a steadying breath. Gemini was a good man. He was a snow leopard. Not a wolf. But Waylon still didn't quite understand why Gemini had no interest in joining their pack, even though he was mated to their healer. Waylon had never had a problem accepting other Were breeds into their rag-tag bunch.

"Thank you for being here for Frost. I recognize how dangerous this new position is for him. If anything had gone wrong..."

Gemini nodded. His long, blond hair bounced with the motion. "I'm aware. You never have to thank me for protecting my mate. But King Jonathan says Celeste chose Frost for this, so I have to believe he'll be okay."

Waylon's gaze moved from Gemini's eerily light blue eyes to the house. He tried to squash the growing jealousy. It seemed he would never have as much as anyone else. He was doomed to be the leader and nothing else. It was a lonely existence.

"Just because you haven't found your mate, that doesn't mean you have to be alone. Audor hasn't talked about anything else since you two started dating."

Despite his best efforts, a smile exploded across his face. Shortly after Frost had come to town, their king had sent a pair of Viking vamps to act as his guards. Audor was one of those vampires. He was a little shorter than Waylon, but at six-five, everyone was. He looked exactly like the Viking he was. Blond-haired and blue eyes. Waylon had to admit he had a thing for that. Still.

"What's the point of wasting time on a pointless relationship?" He had to keep saying that and reminding himself how this would end. Vampires and wolves were a forbidden mating. They could fuck, but they would never be true mates. Vampires belonged to Celeste. Weres were a creation of Odin. Odin would never allow a vampire to sit at his tables in Valhalla. Since fated mates were eternal, there was no future with Audor. That didn't mean they hadn't fucked. Waylon's stomach muscles clenched. Goddess, had they fucked. Waylon had never experienced anything like it. He loved being with Audor, but he couldn't let himself get too attached. This would hurt one day.

A soft chuckle rumbled from Gemini. "It's like you've never met anyone you like just because you do. You could have centuries left until you meet your mate." He paused as if he hated to say the rest. Ultimately, he did. "Or one might not exist for you. If Audor fills your life with happiness, then you should reach for that with both hands." Gemini's gaze slid toward the house. His voice took on a sad edge. "Not everything is fated for everyone."

A huge realization landed on Waylon's head. Gemini and Frost had been blessed beyond words to find their other half, but they would never experience what Frost had just done for Randall and Ashka. He was sure they would be happy nonetheless, but Gemini was right. Not every blessing was meant for everyone. Maybe explosive sex with a drop-dead gorgeous vampire was all that was meant for him. He supposed there were worse fates.

Like every night, Audor kept sentry from a distance. It was Audor's honor to serve his king. He also owed Frost for once saving his life. Shortly after Audor had been sent to Wulfe, Washington to watch over the town's new healer while also keeping an eye out for Lucifer, his brother-in-arms Leif and he had spotted Lucifer leaving Frost's work. They had followed. It seemed Lucifer hadn't appreciated being tailed. He had ripped Audor's leg from his body like plucking wings from a butterfly. If Frost hadn't helped, Audor would have—at the very least—been one-legged now. More likely, he'd be dead. He lost more blood than he could take in. It wouldn't have taken long. He owed Frost for that.

Despite that debt and his orders, and his appreciation of Frost, he was more than happy to pass the duty to Leif for the night. His skin practically itched with the need to see Waylon. The moment he was set free, Audor dissipated and reappeared inside Waylon's living room. Waylon sat kicked back on the couch. His smile showed how unbothered he was by the intrusion. Audor grabbed a chair from the kitchen table and set it facing Waylon. He sat and went to work, massaging Waylon's feet. No one pampered Waylon. Audor wanted the job. His gaze never wavered

18

from Waylon's gorgeous face. He was a sculptor's dream.

"I heard you've had a day."

Waylon's smile grew bigger. "Well, Ashka had a day. I just sat by as a witness."

"That still sounds stressful, considering how the odds are never favorable."

"How was your day?" Waylon always did that. He always turned the subject away from himself, as if he was unimportant. Audor understood why Odin had chosen him to lead this pack. He was selfless.

Audor would let him keep it. "Boring. Thankfully. For the most part, Frost just does his job. As for Lucifer, he pops in and out so quickly, there's no tracking his movements." Audor hated that part.

In his heart, he knew Lucifer would eventually make this town his bitch. While he was grateful for the excuse to be here with Waylon, the waiting was the worst part.

"I imagine Frost is exhausted between his job at the hospital and being the community healer. The Americas' king of vampires sent two of you to watch him while there's only one of him."

Audor nodded. "Mostly, I feel for his mate. They're still newly mated and their time is being stolen."

"At least they have a mate."

There it was. Audor stopped rubbing Waylon's feet. He didn't know how to respond. Audor never did. Mates were everything in their world, but it seemed neither of them had sacrificed enough to be granted that blessing. Audor would be lying if he said he wasn't bitter. He was old. Audor had lived a life of service to the gods. Yet he had no one, and the man he wanted couldn't be his mate. It was soul shattering.

Audor's gaze followed Waylon as he moved from person to person, laughing and talking. He knew everyone inside the tiny bar. Audor saw inside each mind. They all genuinely loved Waylon. Just as he loved them. Being alpha was in his blood and was everything to him. For three months, Audor had been the focus of Waylon's caring nature. He had held Waylon's stare as they made love... heard the regret in his mind that Audor would never be the one. Audor's hand automatically went to his chest, trying to massage away the hole that grew bigger every day. He was in love with Waylon. Audor hadn't meant for it to happen. When he had ended up beneath Waylon that first night under a full moon, he had only sought something he couldn't explain. Audor had needed to let go of his responsibilities and let someone else care for him. He never expected to feel the way he did now when he looked at Waylon.

As if he felt Audor's longing, his head turned. Their gazes met. Those amazing amber eyes took on a very wolf-like sheen. Hunger grew. Waylon crossed the room. A sexy smile touched his lips. Audor's gaze dropped to eye them. Goddess. He ached to feel that mouth on his skin. Waylon took up a scarily large portion of Audor's thoughts. He just wanted to be in Waylon's arms.

Waylon came to stand over him. "Hey there, beautiful."

"Hey." Even Audor heard how happy he was to see Waylon.

Waylon shuffled closer. Promise flashed in his eyes. "Are you on the hunt for your soulmate tonight, or do you want to come home with me?"

A lump formed in Audor's throat. Waylon didn't take them seriously, while he was all Audor thought about. He didn't understand why he kept setting himself on fire for this wolf. Audor should let him go.

Waylon's lips skimmed his cheek before moving to the shell of his ear. "I know what I want you to choose."

A stuttered breath escaped Audor. It seemed he would set himself ablaze at least one more night. Maybe tomorrow, he would walk away. Tonight, he wasn't that strong.

"Come here."

At Waylon's soft command, Audor forced his mind back to the moment and forgot to hurt. That was why he couldn't stop showing up here. Waylon took away the loneliness and frustration. He warmed the bitterness. When they were together, he didn't see them as clearly. His love blinded him. Audor stood and straddled Waylon. The man's animalistic amber eyes kept Audor captivated.

Thank you.

The words sweetly caressed Audor's brain. As a vampire, he could read any lesser being's mind. He tried not to do it as much as possible. It wasn't necessarily a good thing to know people's true opinions. Sometimes, Waylon invaded his mind without warning. It was nice. Audor wouldn't pretend he hadn't heard.

"For what?"

Waylon's sexy smile proved how proud he was to have shoved his way into Audor's thoughts. "For giving me this." He hauled Audor closer. "I'm sorry if I ever make you feel less than. You're not.

I'm so fucking grateful for you wasting your time with me. I recognize you shouldn't."

Audor didn't know if he felt better. Waylon still considered their relationship as wasting time. He stole a kiss and gave himself a minute to think. Audor needed to sort out his feelings. Did he feel better when he was with Waylon? That was what relationships were supposed to be about. He didn't. It hurt his chest being here, and he didn't know why. He shouldn't feel anything. They honestly had only been sleeping together for about five months. Unfortunately, being with Waylon made him realize a person could fall in love with someone not meant for them. All the way in love. He felt dumb as hell and Waylon was right to keep reminding him they weren't meant for this. They weren't. The longer he waited to make a clean break, the more it would hurt. It already hurt. There was only one way to cauterize a wound. Quickly.

Audor swiped his lips across Waylon's and dissipated, ripping out his own heart. They weren't meant to be, and pretending otherwise was killing him. It was best to move along. As Waylon claimed, Audor wasted his time. He wouldn't any longer.

Chapter Two

EVERY SECOND OF HIS conversation with Audor ate at the back of Waylon's mind all day and night. He kept hoping they would cross paths, but no. With Audor working the daylight hours, his powers were dulled. He had to drive like a human, which should have made it easier for Waylon to find him. It was a small town of just over twenty-five hundred residents. Waylon drove around, keeping an eye out for Audor's truck. It didn't seem like there were too many places he could hide, but Wulfe was on the edge of Gifford Pinchot National Forest. That gave Audor over a million and a half acres to disappear. Still, his job was supposed to be shadowing Frost. He shouldn't be too far.

Waylon scanned the hospital parking lot as he walked toward the door. He didn't see Audor or his truck, even though Frost was parked in his usual spot. It took Waylon a few minutes to find Frost, which gave him the excuse he needed to search every corner.

Frost was all smiles—the way he always was—when he saw Waylon headed his way. "Sheriff Black."

"How long are we going to have to be friends before you call me Waylon all the time? Not just when I'm off duty."

A nice-sounding chuckle rumbled from Frost. "I just like making you feel important while you're in uniform."

Despite the way his chest ached, Waylon laughed. "I don't know. At this point, I think I'd feel a lot more special if I wasn't the least bit important any time of the day."

Frost's smile disappeared. He eyed Waylon. While Frost was mostly human, Waylon wasn't sure that was true at all. According to Audor, he had magic in his blood. Waylon had never been sure how much Frost saw in other people. For all he knew, Frost could read everyone's mind.

"Do you want to go to lunch?" Frost's offer caught him off guard, but not in a bad way. He had planned to hang around the hospital and hope he caught Audor. This was better. Audor's responsibility would be in Waylon's care.

"I'd love that. I'll drive."

"Sounds great. Just let me send a text so hospital staff knows to text me if they need anything. Then we can go anywhere you'd like. I'll buy."

Judging by Frost's gorgeous five-bedroom cabin, he could afford it, but Waylon had lived a long time and he could too. Plus, he was the alpha here. "Nah. I've got it."

Frost smiled and shook his head. "You may be the alpha, but you're not my alpha. Let someone else take care of you for once."

Damn. That sounded a hell of a lot like Frost had read his mind. If that was the case, then Frost saw his feelings. He couldn't hide. "I'd like that." No one knew what that confession cost him, but it was Frost. He wasn't just anyone, and Waylon didn't know how to explain that.

Thankfully, Frost didn't let his pride sting. He simply sent his text. When he was done, he met Waylon's stare. "I'm ready when you are."

Together, they headed for the door. Waylon's gaze never stopped moving. He knew if he could just see Audor, talk to him, then he could explain he wasn't good with words. He hadn't meant to insinuate he wasted his time on Audor. Waylon massaged his chest. Fuck. Why was he so dumb? He opened the passenger door for Frost before climbing into his patrol car, ensuring Frost was safe first.

"I can feel your pain."

Waylon's head whipped around at Frost's words.

Frost flashed him a sad smile. "I didn't want to say anything inside where we might be overheard. While I'm not sure about anything that comes with this new role, I know it's growing stronger. I feel when people are hurting. It's like I'm being called to action. I can't really explain it. I just know you're hurting and that I could probably help in some small way. But I need to know what's wrong first, and I'm not sure you care to tell me."

Waylon took a deep breath and started the car. "Let's run through the drive-thru of that new sandwich shop and find a quiet place to talk." While Waylon absolutely did not want to bare his soul, Goddess Celeste had sent Frost to their town for a reason. He would trust in that.

Still, as he ordered their food and then drove to the parking lot of a nearby hiking trail, Waylon couldn't think of what to say or where to start. He picked through every inch of his mind and came up short. Waylon wasn't much of a conversationalist. Talking about his feelings sure as hell was off limits, but he kind of had to.

"I upset Audor and now he's ignoring me." Waylon had spent the entire night and day begging Audor to listen. His texts and mental pleas had gone ignored. He felt only a black spot when he tried to feel him.

Frost munched on the corner of his sandwich while looking lost in thought. It was as if he turned inside himself to find an answer Waylon didn't have. "Tell me a little more."

Waylon wanted to growl at Frost's demand. This was already more than he discussed with anyone else. Still, Waylon took a deep breath and tried to pick a place to start.

"I guess you probably know we've had a bit of a thing since he came to town."

Frost nodded.

Waylon kept going. "I guess I didn't take it too seriously or think he did either, since we can't be mates."

"Why does that matter? I mean, obviously, I know how different a mate feels from just dating someone. But before I met Gemini, and I didn't know he existed, there were times when I still believed I'd been in love. I still had the excitement and passion and turmoil. It just wasn't what I have now, but I hadn't yet experienced this to diminish that. From what Gemini says, not everyone has a mate. If that's the case, then maybe you can feel just as strongly as you do for a mate for anyone you want. Maybe you just get to choose."

Waylon chewed that over. He had to admit the passion with Audor was off the charts. Surely things wouldn't be that way if he had a mate. Maybe Audor didn't have another half either. It was possible they could simply choose each other—like humans choose a life partner. He didn't know.

Waylon shook his head. He had gotten off track. "I guess I've been alive so long and seen so many fated mates that I can't stop believing I'll have that one day. Since meeting Audor, I've swung pretty wildly between happiness and not wanting to get hurt or hurt him when a mate appears for one of us. People are moving here like crazy since they learned we have a healer. I think part of me kind of hoped and feared one of these new arrivals was meant for me. Then again, I'm also terrified maybe they'll be meant for Audor. We're more likely doomed than not." Waylon made a wild gesture. "That's neither here nor there. What I'm getting at is I haven't let him in the way he's done for me. Despite knowing this was likely pointless, he hasn't held anything back. Last night, I decided I'd be the same. He deserves better, but then when I tried to say that, everything came out all wrong. He disappeared and is ignoring me now. I don't know. Maybe it's for the best." Even as he said the words, Waylon tasted the lie. He felt the pain. Waylon didn't want them to end. He wasn't ready to give up Audor.

Frost set his hand on Waylon's arm. Warmth traveled up his arm and settled in his chest. "This is a small town. He can't avoid you forever. Maybe Gemini and I can have a small barbecue this weekend and get you both under the same roof. You can kidnap him... during the day, anyhow."

They exchanged a smile that turned into a laugh. Waylon felt better. He had a plan. The weekend was still a couple of days away. Maybe he would manage to corner Audor before then. If not, Frost's plan sounded like a win. He would take what he could get.

Audor hadn't told Waylon, since he hadn't really gotten a chance, but with more vampires headed their way, Audor didn't have to spend every single day shadowing Frost any longer. He had extra help now. He could take some days off a week. Audor had planned to surprise Waylon today by sticking to him like glue and enjoying some time together. He hadn't expected things to end so quickly. Now he had unexpected time off and nothing to do but think.

When Gemini had put his home up for sale to move in with Frost, Audor had quickly bought the place before it slipped away. The house was small, but he was only one vamp, and the garage was huge. Plus, the two hundred acres surrounding him gave him the illusion of the old days before the air stank of pollution all hours of the day. He had to admit people smelled better, making his meals easier. Not all progress was bad. Audor also enjoyed a cozy bed and heat in the winter. Air in the summer too, truth be told. Okay, so he liked more than he hated about today's world, but he was still happy with his purchase.

Between guarding Frost and spending his nights in Waylon's bed, he hadn't gotten around to doing the things he wanted with the property. Audor focused on that now, hoping to keep himself sane. The automatic bay door system on the garage didn't work, so Audor fixed that first. From there, he went to work on a stack of lumber. He built shelves and a table. The daylight hours might weaken him, but he was still faster and stronger than any human.

He kept his hands busy and made his muscles scream. The hole in his chest wouldn't let him forget it was there, but Audor would be damned if he dwelled on it.

"Would you like some help?"

Audor spun so fast, he almost tweaked his back. He had been so focused on not thinking, he hadn't felt Riku coming. "Holy shit. Where did you come from?"

Riku smiled. His skin had the glow of summer, even though they were just heading into spring. His messy dark hair made his almost yellow eyes pop. Those eyes danced with laughter at his expense. "Snakes are pretty silent."

"I fucking guess. You nearly made me throw my back out. I'm old, you know."

"Me too."

Audor wanted to ask how old, but Riku likely didn't recall. He was a godling—created, used, and discarded by Jörmungandr. Riku had probably seen the birth of several planets. He looked twenty.

Riku's gaze moved over him, openly studying his shirtless state. "Judging by the layer of dirt on your skin, I'm guessing you've been at this a while."

With a shrug, Audor looked away. "Yeah. Well. I've put off a lot of chores since coming to town."

Dressed from head to toe in black, Riku pulled his coat closed tighter. "I suppose you're accustomed to this weather."

It was obvious he tried making conversation about anything at all. Audor wondered if Riku was lonely. Unlike Audor or the Weres of this town, there was no one else like him. Audor suddenly felt less alone. While there were creatures who looked like him and acted like him, Audor had never truly fit. He wanted to wake up with the sun and drink coffee with his mate. Audor wanted to go to bed each night and snuggle into the warmth. He wanted something he hadn't quite captured in all his long life.

Audor moved to the corner and grabbed a large space heater. He plugged it in and set a chair beside it. After cranking the dial to the highest setting, he motioned for Riku to sit. "Please? To me, this weather closely mimics Sweden. I've spent countless nights sleeping in the snow. This place is nothing. I imagine where you're from is not the same."

While wearing a grateful smile, Riku sat. He leaned close to the heat. "Nothing is the same here, but the cold is the worst." Riku hesitated. "And possibly the emotions. Everything is muted in the heavens. Here, well, sometimes, I'm suffocated by my own mind."

In Audor's world, it was rare for anyone to speak so openly about their feelings. While Leif had been his best friend for hundreds of years, they were still warriors. They weren't supposed to feel too much. It was nice to be around someone so open.

"You'd think it would be the other way around. The gods are so powerful. It seems like they should feel more."

"That's exactly why heaven is kept intentionally muted. Powerful emotion leads to passionate disagreements."

"How else is it different there? Why would you choose this mountain? I have so many questions."

Riku laughed, but there was no humor in the sound. "Sometimes choices aren't as many as you think. Sometimes, what looks like free will isn't truly free at all."

A sad smile tugged at Audor's lips. "I'm certain it's more often than sometimes."

They shared a smile.

Audor went back to work with Riku watching him. His presence was comforting. Audor needed that today.

"It seems Frost is planning a small bar-becue this weekend. You should bring a date."

A pain sliced through Audor. He tried hiding it with a laugh. "Are you offer-ing?"

"Are you trying to get both legs ripped off?"

Audor laughed for real. They both knew the real and biggest reason Audor had been sent to this town was because of Riku. He was Lucifer's unclaimed mate. The only reason Audor knew was be-cause Jonathan would never leave him blind to what he was up against. No one knew what would happen when the day came that Lucifer's patience snapped. Riku might be Jörmungandr's discard-ed creation, but he was his creation nonetheless. Some believed Jörmungan-dr would be the one who brought on the end of the world. Between that and Lu-cifer's hatred of everything and every-one, their mating could mean the end of times. It might also mean a dozen other things or nothing at all. If Audor actually flirted with Riku, he would like-ly be dead before the words fully left his ripped-out tongue. It was scary how much that fate didn't sound so bad.

"Sometimes, I build a huge, roaring fire on the mountain." Riku sounded so qui-et and low that Audor had to stop and stare. Riku looked at nothing as he spoke, as if only seeing the images in his head. It looked as if fire danced in his eyes. Audor had never been more awed, and he served the golden king. "I'll sit as closely as possible, telling myself the snake inside me needs the relief the warmth brings." Riku looked his way. The embers of fire glowed hotter and danced faster. "But I know the truth. I'm trying to decide if I should step into it. What would happen if I did? Would I die with honor the way the vampire do? Maybe nothing at all would happen beyond ruining a set of clothes. Or per-haps I'll set Lucifer free, and this town can take a breath with the threat of me gone. Only the not knowing stops me." The embers died. "A lot of your kind have found a home here. You should pick one to go with you to Frost's. I daresay a lot of us feel the same weariness from the unending march of time."

A sad smile tugged at Audor's lips. "Maybe I will. Wisdom is welcome wherever it comes from. I appreciate the advice. For the record, though, fear of Lucifer wouldn't stop me from pursuing you if my heart was whole."

A smile snapped to Riku's lips. "I don't doubt it. Now, tell me your plan for this garage so I can help. My life is tedious as hell. I'm game for anything."

A warmth spread through Audor's chest. For the first time since his move, Audor didn't feel either alone or like he waited for the other shoe to drop. He could choose to be Riku's friend. That was a choice that was his and real. He would start there. Then Audor would take back his life. He used to be someone else before the years of loneliness crushed him. Audor would find that man again. He didn't need a wolf to survive.

Chapter Three

WAYLON'S NERVES WERE A complete
mess. After days of not seeing Audor, and the feeling of going out of his
head worsening by the second, Waylon
turned up first at Frost's for the barbecue. He pretended to be fine. The way
he always did. Waylon chopped vegeta-
bles and chatted. His face hurt from the
faked smiles. Then, one by one, other
people arrived. Waylon sat in the corner
with a beer and held his breath each
time the door opened. Everyone Frost invited, including a few he hadn't, had already shown. No Audor. He waited ten

more minutes and then headed outside to hover over Jacen at the grill.

Jacen flashed him a smile. "Hey. You look tired. Do you ever get a break?"

Waylon tried to hide his emotions, even though it would be impossible with Jacen. His wife Deidra and he were fairies. They could read and control the minds of animals. That was the biggest reason the people of Wulfe had tried to steer clear of them when they moved to town. But Frost had immediately struck up a friendship with the pair, and they had slowly grown on everyone else.

"There's only one of me, but I try."

Jacen nodded. "Do you mind watching these burgers for a second while I grab a beer?"

A genuine smile snapped to Waylon's lips. Fairies asking for a favor was a genuine honor. No matter how small. "Sure. Take your time."

Waylon took over Jacen's spot and focused on the chore. It was nice to empty his mind for a second. Jacen was back too soon. He had a beer in each hand.

He handed one to Waylon. "Here."

Waylon nodded his appreciation. While everyone knew not to accept food or drinks from fairies, Jacen had manned the grill at every one of these get-togethers in the past six months. None of them had gotten stuck in the fairy world yet or lost their ability to eat anything other than the guy's cooking. Waylon assumed they were safe.

A familiar voice caressed his ears, as if Waylon had been waiting to hear its tune. "Sorry we're late. Fen had a meeting with the king this morning he couldn't miss."

Waylon tempered himself as he turned. His fur already stood on end. He feared himself when he saw how closely the Fen guy stood to Audor.

Audor was all smiles.

Frost looked as if he fought himself, swinging between being a proper host and upset on Waylon's behalf. Audor had brought a fucking date.

"I don't think we've met," Frost said, obviously trying to cover his reaction.

Fen held out his hand. "Fen Baird."

Fuck. He had a Scottish accent.

Frost shook. "Frost Leo."

Fen dipped his chin. "I know. You're the reason I'm here."

Audor jumped in, as if Fen needed him to clarify. "Fen is one of Scotland's king's personal guards."

"Was," Fen clarified with a laugh. "Your safety is a top priority now. To the heed-ful seldom comes harm."

Frost officially looked uncomfortable. Gemini came to his rescue and Audor led Fen to the nearby lawn chairs. It was a nice day, and everyone felt the same itch of spring on the horizon. Waylon openly studied Fen. He was tall, with red hair and unnaturally bright green eyes. As much as it hurt his chest to admit it, he was a gorgeous guy. He was also a vampire, exactly as Audor needed. Waylon chugged his beer and headed inside for another. He couldn't watch Audor be with someone else. He grabbed another beer from the fridge and stood at the kitchen counter, staring at nothing.

Warm arms encircled him. Lips brushed his nape, sending chill bumps down his spine. Waylon's eyes fell closed at the sensation. His chest hurt. While the humans in this town weren't technically part of his pack, they were still his responsibility as their sheriff. He had lost two today in a horrific car accident. Teens, driving too fast for the lack of experience. Their parents' faces haunted Waylon's mind. Audor's touch soothed him.

"You're a good man. This town is obviously favored by the gods to have you, but you need a break sometimes too." Audor's lips skimmed his skin with every word, making Waylon's breathing deepen.

"I wouldn't even know where to start."

He felt Audor smile against his neck. *"That's okay. I've got you."* Audor urged him to turn and stepped into his arms. Before Waylon had time to decide where things were headed, his feet were swept across the floor. Music fired to life. Their dance was slow at first before the music changed to something fast. Before long, laughter bounced from the walls of his tiny kitchen as he tried to keep up with Audor. The sound was silenced when Audor's mouth covered his.

Waylon had never felt so much, and he didn't understand why.

"I take it you're no longer seeing Audor."

The words ripped Waylon from one of the few good memories he kept for only himself. He glanced over. A vampire who had come with Leif leaned his hip against the counter and studied Waylon, waiting for a response.

"Sorry. I don't remember your name." It was all Waylon could think to say. Obviously, he had become the talk of the town already.

"I'll bet. You were with Audor when we met. I don't think you even looked away from him to catch my name, much less match it with a face."

Gods. He hurt. Why had this vampire come to torture him?

"It's Stone."

Waylon had a hard time looking at the guy's eyes. All vampires had an unnatural glow that saw too much. "That's modern for a vampire." He had nothing to talk about.

"Or just unoriginal for peasant parents."

Despite everything, a chuckle escaped Waylon at the humor in Stone's voice. Waylon sipped his beer.

Stone took it from him and set it aside. "You don't know much about matters of the heart, do you? Otherwise, you'd be outside with me, fighting fire with fire."

Waylon finally met Stone's stare at the comment. Interest flashed back at him. Waylon didn't think it was personal. He had a feeling vamps were just a horny lot.

Stone didn't stop. "Sometimes, people think they're through until that jealousy stirs." He took a step closer, invading Waylon's space. "You're just as capable of that as he is." Stone's gaze moved to Waylon's lips. "More so, I'd say."

"I'll get a beer later."

Waylon's gaze shot to the kitchen doorway just in time to see Audor's retreating form.

A low chuckle slipped from Stone. "Now it's a party." He handed Waylon back his beer. "Come on, sexy. Don't let him see you hurt." He took Waylon's free hand and headed for the backyard. Waylon went with his heart in his throat. He didn't know what was happening to his life, but he let it happen. Stone was right. Two could play this game. If Audor didn't want him, someone else would. He wouldn't play the fool.

A hot coal burned inside Audor's gut. It felt a little like jealousy. The night became like a tennis match. Each time Waylon served him a helping of jealousy, Audor hit back just as hard. By the time darkness fell and everyone had drunk way more than their share of alcohol, Stone sat on Waylon's knee and Fen stared at Audor like his next meal. Things were a mess. He felt like all eyes were on them, waiting to see who broke first. It was a nightmare.

Audor tried tuning out everyone's thoughts. Waylon's hurt, anger, and determination to punish him was beating at Audor's brain. He couldn't be the only vampire who felt it. Audor had never experienced such deep hatred focused his way... and Lucifer had ripped off his leg.

"I can feel your hunger."

Audor tore his gaze away from where Waylon rubbed Stone's back. He focused on Fen. "What?"

A wicked smile stretched Fen's lips. "You're hungry. When was the last time you fed?"

Audor searched his mind. He was an ancient. Audor could go weeks without feeding. Since he started sleeping with Waylon, he hadn't drunk from anyone else. Waylon's blood was strong. An alpha's blood held him longer than any human's or other vampire's would. He hadn't even thought of blood in a while. Now that Fen mentioned it, he was starving. He had just ignored the sensation. The thought of sinking his fangs into anyone other than Waylon hurt his chest. He swore he felt Waylon's stare, as if he too suddenly felt Audor's need to feed.

Fen stood and took his hand. "Come on. We'll step out of sight."

Audor allowed Fen to lead him to the side of the house where no one could see. Darkness shadowed them, but Audor's perfect night vision showed him everything.

Fen backed him against the cabin. The rough wall met his shoulder blades. Fen stalked him, closing the gap between them. His fangs peeked out, as if he was the one getting ready to bite. Audor could practically smell Fen's lust. He begged for Audor's bite. His pulse beat in Audor's ears. He leaned closer—like a moth being drawn to the flame. Audor couldn't resist the call.

An angry growl rent the air.

Fen went flying backward.

Audor blinked in confusion, still under the spell of his needs.

An enraged alpha was there in all his glory. He was terrifying, even knowing vampires were technically the stronger species. Waylon was still the top dog in this town. His wrath was epic.

Leif held Fen back. Fen kept trying to dissipate and escaped the hold to get at Waylon. Leif simply stuck with him every step of the way. They had been best friends for centuries. Leif wouldn't let Fen get involved in this.

Fury filled glowing yellow eyes focused on him. "You dare sink your fangs into someone else."

Audor blinked. It hit him. He was enraged too. Waylon had a lot of nerve. "My fangs are mine. You didn't want them. I was wasting your time, and I remedied that for you. You have no right to do this shit."

He found Waylon in his space and hovering over him, looking ready to tear him apart. "You chose that. I didn't. You know I'm bad with words and you wouldn't hear me. Those fangs belong to me, and I will kill that vampire if you touch him."

Frustration welled inside Audor. Waylon said the things Audor had wanted to hear before it had been too late, but it was now. He had already broken Audor.

"You want them? Fine." He grabbed two handfuls of Waylon's shirt and lifted him from the ground. Audor spun, slamming Waylon against the wall. Waylon's lust hit him. He enjoyed the rough treatment. Audor was furious. He wanted Waylon to hurt the way he had been hurting Audor for months, but he knew Waylon would have to feel the same about him for that to happen, and he didn't. He didn't love Audor the way Audor loved him.

Waylon's eyes widened, as if he heard his thoughts.

Audor didn't give a shit about anything any longer. He was done. Without warning or easing the pain with his mind, Audor tore into Waylon's throat and drank. As blood filled his mouth and he swallowed, Audor experienced an odd tug in his chest. His muscles relaxed. His motions became more loving than angry. When Waylon moaned, Audor hated himself for that. He retracted his fangs and licked the wound, sealing it, before pulling away. Audor took a step back. He opened his mouth to let Waylon know this would be the last time. His gaze locked on the scar forming on Waylon's neck. Shock rendered him mute before pain sliced through him. It couldn't be. Waylon couldn't be his mate.

Audor's gaze snapped to Waylon's.

Waylon panted like he had run a marathon.

He didn't want this. Waylon hadn't loved him without that scar. Now, if he said the words, it would only be because of it. Plus, this shouldn't even be possible. There had to be a mistake. He couldn't live with that. Audor would walk into the fire. His heart couldn't take this. Without a single thought, he dissipated, leaving the other half of his soul behind.

Chapter Four

SIX WEEKS EARLIER...

Celeste picked her way through the halls of Valhalla, stepping over drunken men with her head held high. It wasn't in her to beg, and she wouldn't, but she knew in her gut when something should be. Her glimpses into the future with Audor had always been hazy, and she had never been sure why. She had suspected it had something to do with her brother, since Audor had been destined to end up in Wulfe. Now she saw it. Audor was meant to love a wolf.

Only once since the beginning of time had Celeste found a loophole to bring a wolf and vampire together. A human had been fated to end up with either, so he had gotten both. Odin had been furious with the loss of an alpha. Now here she was again with another alpha on the hook. Odin might very well go to war over this one. She had no idea how this conversation would end. But, as always, she had a plan.

Odin huffed at the sight of her. "No. Whatever it is, no. You never come here unless you want something, and I never like it."

Celeste laughed. Despite all their differences, Celeste liked him better than other gods. They had never fought. Their creations had always banded together.

She didn't understand why he couldn't see how much stronger they could be as a team.

"Don't worry. I haven't come to ask for anything." She held up the dice she carried. "I've come to wager you for it."

The eye Odin still possessed sparkled with laughter. "You've come to lose, eh?" He motioned toward the chair across from him and waved for everyone to leave them. "Sit and say what it is you're after, then."

If Odin didn't already know, it showed how little attention he paid to his packs. "Waylon Black's soul."

A roar of obnoxious and obviously faked laughter echoed from the walls of the great hall. "You must be joking. What is it you plan to lose, then? You've already stolen one alpha from me."

"I didn't steal Raff. You were handsomely rewarded."

"Recompense, not reward. I think that's what you meant."

Celeste waved away his words. She sat and tucked a strand of her shining blond hair behind her ear. Celeste eyed him, sizing him up. Odin was a massive guy with scars and muscles for days. He had seen some things. Odin was a warrior through and through. Celeste wasn't sure she had much to offer he would accept, but this was too important not to try.

She dumped the dice on the table. "Best of three. If I win, I get Waylon. You win, and you can have a night with me."

Odin's eyebrows shot up. It was obvious she had shocked him speechless. No one got a night with her.

Celeste couldn't hold his stare. She humbled herself for no one, but she was in love with falling in love. Celeste couldn't break Waylon or Audor by pairing them with anyone else. She picked up the dice, ready to toss them if he was ready to deal.

Odin's giant hand covered hers, stopping the motion.

Celeste lifted her gaze.

Odin stared at her in a kind way she had never experienced from him. "Say you want one night with me for real, and not on some lost wager. If that's true, I'll give you more than Waylon. We can discuss joining our clans."

Her pride pricked, making her want to deny any type of true desire. Celeste's mouth didn't give a fuck about her pride. It beat her good sense to the punch. "I want you for real." That was saying a lot, considering how muted emotions were here.

Odin sat back hard, as if shock took the wind from his sails. "Then you should stay."

Celeste felt the way those words shifted everything for the future. She practical-ly felt history reshape. "Okay."

Like that, her fate was sealed.

Present day...

Waylon couldn't stop staring at himself in the mirror. The scar on his neck was an even bigger miracle than he ever dreamed, except it was also a nightmare. Audor had disappeared again. There was a hole in the center of Waylon's chest, and he had no idea who to ask if this was real. Maybe he had just gotten so old, his scars finally showed.

He had no clue. All he knew was this shouldn't be possible. Yet he felt Audor missing from him like a limb and he realized now he had since the first night Audor ended things.

I can feel you missing from me. Please come back.

He kept making the silent plea, only to be met with more emptiness. Waylon had no idea where Audor had gone, but it was as if he was dead. He couldn't feel Audor at all. It was suffocating.

I'm the alpha here. I can't leave to find you. Please.

Waylon begged no one, but he couldn't stop. There was no way Audor understood the place he was in. When Waylon had accepted his position to lead this pack, he had known it meant he had to stay with them. The only way he could chase Audor was if he stepped down. The temptation was massive. He had given enough. When would it be his turn? Waylon mentally flipped through the list of possible replacements. They were all too young. Too hot headed. Fuck. He hated this.

"You didn't show up for work. People are worried after your fight last night."

Waylon met Riku's stare in the mirror. "You just popping into people's homes now?"

Riku flashed a smile. "Godling. I do what I want. Plus, I was genuinely concerned. Audor marked your skin and took your blood, but you haven't taken his. That's a dark place to be in. You belong to him, but he doesn't yet belong to you. I had to make sure you weren't planning something stupid. The pain is massive."

Waylon moved away from the mirror and grabbed a shirt. He angrily pulled it on. It seemed he had to go to fucking work or this whole goddamn town would be at his door—like he wasn't allowed one damn night of losing his temper. "What would you know about it?"

Riku followed him from the bathroom into the bedroom. He sat on the bed. "A lot, actually. I have an unclaimed mate."

That froze Waylon in his tracks. "I hadn't heard that."

A soft chuckle rumbled from Riku. "This gossipy town doesn't know everything."

Finding out Riku had an unclaimed mate had shocked him for half a second, but he landed on enraged in the end. "You have a mate and they're just out there hurting because... why? That's a shitty thing to do to a person." He knew he was projecting, but damn. Waylon didn't understand why people were handed blessings straight from Celeste and turned their backs. How could Riku do that? It was cruel. Just like what Audor did to him now. The more he thought about it, the angrier he got. Vampires and Weres weren't supposed to be possible, but they were. Defying all odds, Audor belonged to him. This was massive. It was beautiful history-making. This was the most hateful thing anyone had ever done to him, denying him love. How fucking dare Riku so casually speak of doing the same?

"It's Lucifer."

Waylon sat. Thankfully, the bed was there to catch him. One second, he stood. The next, he was on his ass. His gaze locked on Riku and wouldn't budge. He was serious. It was in his eyes. "Holy shit."

A sad smile touched Riku's lips. He looked away. His throat moved on what looked to be a painful swallow. "Yeah. That was pretty much my reaction too."

Waylon's problems were all the way forgotten. "What do you plan to do?"

Riku's hands rose and fell, landing on his lap. "I've been round and round in my head and I don't know. But I know I won't make it much longer one way or the other. I'm old and strong, but this is beating me. Every day is like setting myself on fire. But what am I supposed to do?"

Waylon had no idea. What would happen if Riku claimed Lucifer? The prospects were endless and horrific. Another thought sneaked in. Riku was the best person he knew. Maybe he had just projected his anger on the guy, but Riku watched out for this town every bit as much as Waylon. He certain-ly prayed for them more than anyone. With an open line to the gods, that meant a lot. No one with that much heart would be given a challenge he couldn't handle.

"You should claim him."

Riku's gaze shot his way. "You realize that could mean the end of everything. I'm a descendant of Jörmungandr. Lucifer's future is shrouded in darkness, hidden from even Celeste. Jörmungandr has always been predicted to end the world. This could be the catalyst. Do you think Jörmungandr would approve of this match?"

Waylon shrugged. "I don't know anything about the guy, but Celeste wouldn't have chosen you if she didn't believe in you. She's obviously still seeing a future—no matter what you choose. So, obviously, the world isn't nearing its end." That seemed pretty cut and dry to Waylon. If Celeste saw all except her brother, things obviously worked out. Surely Riku would know if she saw the end of the rest of them.

Riku looked away again. "Maybe everything works out because I choose death."

Waylon's shoulders fell. He hadn't considered that, but obviously, Riku had. Without thinking, he took Riku's hand and squeezed, bringing Riku's gaze his way. Waylon waited until he had Riku's attention. "What do you think Lucifer would do if you chose that path?" Waylon was genuinely curious. It was obvious this was the true reason Lucifer kept showing up in his town. There was no way Lucifer didn't know Riku was his. Lucifer was known for his greed. Waylon couldn't imagine what would happen if a gift from his sister slipped through his fingers. Truly, he couldn't picture it. He had no idea how someone evil like Lucifer would view this.

Riku held his stare. "I can't say for sure, but I have a bad feeling I know. That's why I haven't done it."

The weight of the situation fully fell on Waylon's shoulders. If Riku chose death, Lucifer would raze this town to the ground, but likely the rest of the world would be saved. Sometimes, there were no good choices. Only choices. One day very soon, Riku would have to decide, and it would affect them all.

Audor roamed the perimeter of King Jonathan's Louisiana hidden fortress. It was endless acres of magical land that expanded as needed. It couldn't be found on any map or seen at all unless your name was on a guest list or personally invited. Thankfully, Audor's name was on the list. He needed the peaceful respite.

The moonlight poured down on him, enveloping him in its healing hold. His mate was out there, under this same moon. Audor rubbed his chest. He heard Waylon's thoughts. His pleas. He knew Waylon would never beg anyone. Yet he did Audor. It was heartbreaking. An alpha should have never been brought so low. Waylon didn't deserve this. He should have been given a wolf's mate to run beneath the full moon with him. Now Waylon was stuck feeling more than he should for someone he hadn't wanted beyond sex. Even then, he had considered being with Audor as a waste of time. How was Audor supposed to return to Wulfe? Everyone knew Waylon hadn't been his when Audor marked his skin. He looked like a fucking fool. Topping things off, this match shouldn't even be. Odin would likely see him dead first. He kept waiting for the lightning to strike.

"Your thoughts are exhausting. I'm having a hard time understanding why Celeste wanted this for you." Audor spun. At the sight of the gigantic, scarred warrior in an eye patch, Audor immediately hit his knees. Odin wasn't his god, but he was still a god, deserving of honor.

"Stand up, boy. I'm too old to be cricking my neck like this."

Audor slowly moved to his feet. He didn't know what to say. This was a position he never even entertained. He licked his lips. "Sorry. I don't actually know how to greet you. How may I be of service?"

"You can get your ass back to Wulfe and accept the gift Celeste has given you, dumbass." Odin pinched the spot between his eyes. "I can't believe I'm doing this. First time in my entire existence, I thought with my dick." He muttered the words under his breath. Odin dropped his hand. His one bright blue eye pinned Audor in place. "Waylon was handpicked by me as the northwest pack leader. He's a wolf of worth. You insult me and Celeste by turning your back on this honor you've been bestowed. Goddess knows I wouldn't have chosen this." He paused and stared at nothing. "Not that I have regrets. The opposite, in fact. I should get back." Odin disappeared as quickly as he appeared, leaving Audor reeling.

"Holy shit. Was that Odin?"

Audor forced his head to turn toward the voice. Tam was nearby, riding his husband's shoulders in an attempt to climb a tree. The pair were frozen, staring at where Odin had stood only moments earlier, and proving Audor hadn't imagined things.

"It would seem so." Even Audor heard the shock in his voice.

Tam visibly swallowed. "He's much bigger than I expected."

Audor nodded, feeling frozen by the experience.

"You should do as he says."

Audor nodded again, wondering if his mind had finally snapped.

"You know, you could just have your mate take you up the tree with his mind, right?" Audor didn't know why he said the words. It was like his mouth needed to do something while his brain sat frozen.

Tam blinked. "I know. This isn't about being in the tree. It's about living the experience of the climb. We're making a happy memory."

Fuck. He was so right. All along, his love had never been about ultimately becoming Waylon's mate. He had adored every second of the experience of just being with Waylon with zero hope of this miracle. But now, he had reached a goal he hadn't even known possible, and he got to keep this love forever. He would always know his love was real, regardless of this blessing because he had loved Waylon even when there had been no hope. Each second the shock thawed, the bigger the truth got. This was real. It was really real. Celeste and Odin had chosen them. Holy shit. He was floored. What was he supposed to do now?

Chapter Five

EXHAUSTION WEIGHED HEAVILY ON Frost's shoulders. His job at the hospital, coupled with what felt like nonstop back-to-back emergencies with the supernatural community, had him half dead. He had no idea how he was any use to anyone, especially Gemini. Frost fought a wave of sadness. He knew Gemini would feel it.

I love you so much. Just come home. I'll fix it.

Frost smiled as Gemini's voice brushed his mind. He loved the man he had mar–

ried so fucking much. Frost wanted to do better by him. He deserved more. Just ten more minutes in the car and they would be together.

"For fuck's sake. Just quit the hospital and work on-call for the community. You act as if the world is ending." Lucifer laughed at his own bad joke.

Frost shook his head at Lucifer's sudden appearance in his passenger seat. "I'd leave the hospital in a lurch. From what I gather, they had a hard time finding a doctor willing to move here before they found me."

"First off, so? How's that your problem? Second, you're such a strange little man."

A bark of laughter burst from Frost. He didn't know why, but he genuinely liked Lucifer. That was likely the dumbest thing on the planet, and it had nothing to do with Lucifer literally being the most beautiful creature in existence. He was caustic and self-proclaimed evil. But if Lucifer wanted anything from him, he hadn't revealed his hand yet, and it was honestly refreshing. Lately, it felt like everyone wanted something. Frost tried keeping up his end of the conversation through the fatigue.

"First off, it'd become my problem the moment someone I love can't get help because the hospital is short staffed. Secondly, I know I'm odd, but what the fuck? What did I do to you?"

"In the first place, you're not scared of me. Second, you didn't even startle when I popped in."

Frost shook his head again. He didn't understand Lucifer. "I felt you coming, and it's like you want me to be scared. Aren't you tired of everyone's fear? That sounds draining."

Lucifer was so quiet, Frost might have thought he disappeared if he couldn't see the golden skin from the corner of his eye and smell the faint scent of a campfire mixed with melting marshmallows.

"Melting marshmallows?" Lucifer snorted.

Frost watched the road and smiled. "Yeah. If you don't like what you hear, then don't read my thoughts."

"I love what I hear. That's why I can't stop."

Silence filled the car following Lucifer's confession. It wasn't uncomfortable. Just quiet, which was nice, honestly. Frost was so fucking tired.

Lucifer touched him. That had never happened before. It was just his arm, but it surprised Frost. He got the feeling Lucifer didn't touch many people. His touch was hot. It sent a warm jolt up his arm. His fatigue fell away. Frost recognized Lucifer had taken it from him, healing him in some small way.

"Thank you."

Lucifer snorted again. "Don't thank me. It was purely selfish. You're not giving me your full attention."

A soft chuckle escaped Frost. Lucifer was right. They didn't see each other often. He should make the most of it.

"Would you like to see me more often?" The question came out quietly, surprising Frost in its vulnerability.

He purposefully kept his mind blank. Frost didn't want Lucifer to run. "That depends. Do you plan to destroy this town?"

"That depends."

Well. It was an answer. "On what?"

"My mate lives here."

Frost pulled over and put his SUV in park. He turned in his seat and gave Lucifer his full attention. "Go on."

A laugh that sent chills down Frost's spine caressed Frost's ears. "I can't believe this is what finally shocked you."

"You can't believe this surprised me? Are you joking?" Frost was fucking blown away. He felt like a gossipy teen, wanting to know every detail.

"Rightfully, he doesn't want me."

"Why rightfully? I'd think anyone would be blown away to be paired with you."

A wicked smile hovered on Lucifer's lips. "You would think that. You're an idiot."

Frost huffed and started the SUV. It died before he could shift into drive. He looked Lucifer's way. There was no doubt he was the reason Frost's car was suddenly dead.

"That wasn't an insult to your intelligence. You're dumb when it comes to people... or beings. However you choose to look at this, you've got no sense of survival. I could kill you at any second." Little flames danced inside Lucifer's eyes as if he pictured doing just that or tried frightening Frost.

Frost shrugged. "Statistically, anything could kill me at any moment. If I'm dead, who'll sit and talk to you?"

"My mate, even though he resents every second."

"Who is it? Is there some way I can help?" Frost didn't know what he could do, but he wanted to try. Maybe it was the healing magic in his blood that Jonathan claimed he carried, calling out for Frost to act. Frost didn't think that was it. He thought maybe he wanted to help a friend.

A huge smile exploded across Lucifer's face, obviously still in his thoughts. "Are we doing this teen style? Will you call him and ask him if he likes me while pretending I'm not sitting right here?"

Frost laughed as he pictured doing exactly that. Without thinking, he grabbed Lucifer's hand and held it. "This will work out. I feel it."

Lucifer held his stare. His light blue eyes looked even more intense than usual.

His long blond hair seemed to shimmer even brighter. He didn't let go. In fact, he lightly squeezed Frost's hand. "You should go. Your mate is panicking because he can't feel you."

A shot hit Frost in the chest at the thought of Gemini hurting in any way. "Promise you'll see me again."

"Always." He was gone in an instant, as if he had never been there. Frost blinked, and he sat inside his SUV in his driveway, as if Lucifer had dropped him there. Gemini's panic hit him.

I'm outside, baby. It's okay.

The relief and love that hit him had tears filling Frost's eyes. Poor Lucifer. Someone out there denied him this. The rejection had to be gut-wrenching. He prayed whoever this mate was; he realized what he was doing and fixed things. No one deserved this. Not even the devil.

Waylon stared down at the perfect bundle in his arms. Ashka's baby looked just like her. She slept peacefully while Waylon studied her tiny features. She would be a red wolf like her mother.

"Have you decided on a name?"

Ashka paused in the middle of folding clothes. "Ashka is a family name, passed down through the women in my family. As much as I hate breaking tradition, I loathe the idea of calling my daughter by my name. So, we chose a compromise. Randall's dad's name is Lee. We went with Ashlee."

"That's a good name. She looks like an Ashlee." Waylon stood and gently placed her in the bassinet. "Thank you for allowing me to visit. I worried about you."

Ashka eyed him. Her gaze moved over his mark, showing him as mated. "I worry about you. You don't seem happy for someone newly mated. Not that I know anything about it. I haven't left the house to hear any town gossip."

"Don't think about me. You have too much on your plate." He sat on the opposite side of her pile of laundry and started folding. "Where's your useless man? He should be doing this for you."

Ashka laughed. "He's asleep. Don't be too hard on him. He stayed up all night with Ashlee so I could sleep."

Waylon nodded, humming his approval. He wouldn't hear of any laziness in his pack. They all worked together. That was how packs survived. They sat in silence, folding clothes. He tried hard to keep his mind blank. The reason he had come here was half out of duty and partially from a need to focus on something beyond himself. He didn't have the luxury of letting Audor destroy him.

"Have you tried flowers?"

Ashka's question pulled him from his thoughts about not thinking. "What?"

"For your mate. When I first met Randall, he gathered a bunch of wildflowers from the field to bring to me. You should take your mate flowers."

That was one hundred percent a wolf thing. They loved flowers and pretty rocks. He doubted vampires gave a shit about such things. Audor was a Viking, after all. "Thanks for the suggestion." The more he thought about it, the less ridiculous the idea sounded. Maybe not flowers, but Waylon hadn't tried wooing Audor. He had simply accepted Audor's sexual favors and comfort. Had he ever given Audor the same peace? Likely not. The idea of caring for his mate grew, making the wolf inside him grumble with possessive pride. Audor was his. He was an alpha's mate. Audor was owed all the nice words and attention. He deserved licks and gifts. Just more of everything than he had gotten.

Waylon finished helping Ashka with her chore and stood. "It was good seeing you. If you need anything, let me know."

A sweet smile stared up at him from the couch. "I will, and same. Whenever you're ready, I'd love to meet your mate."

Waylon dipped his chin. "Have a good one." Eventually, the entire pack would expect him to formally introduce his mate. The longer he waited, the more people would talk. He walked away with his mind stuck on how to make Audor happy. Waylon cared way more about that than pleasing anyone else. He had felt Audor's return last night from wherever he had been hidden. While Waylon had wanted to continue begging Audor to come to him, he hadn't. Now Waylon was grateful for it. He knew where Audor was and he shouldn't have to come to Waylon. For once, Audor would be the chased one. An evil smile stretched Waylon's lips. The wolf inside relished the idea of catching his other half. Audor didn't stand a chance.

Audor wasn't sure why he still didn't go to Waylon. He was home. Audor felt his other half every second of the day. He wasn't upset any longer. Seeing Odin had definitely impressed upon him how much of a miracle this was, but every time he thought about going to Waylon, something inside him couldn't do it. He had always gone to Waylon. He didn't want to this time. Waylon had embarrassed him at Frost's gathering. He didn't feel good when he thought of that night. Audor had marked Waylon's skin, claiming him in Waylon's customs, but Waylon had never drunk Audor's blood. He hadn't claimed Audor. Something about them just didn't feel settled. While Audor had no desire to put Waylon behind him, he needed more than a 'well, this is our life now because

Celeste says so.' He wanted to be fucking wanted. For real.

A knock at the door pulled Audor from the rabbit hole he kept falling into. He felt him. Waylon was on the other side. Audor was on his feet with his hand wrapped around the doorknob before he could stop himself. He took a breath and pulled the door open.

Waylon looked like hell. He also looked unsure of his welcome. Audor's chest hurt. Why couldn't Waylon love him for real? Audor had given him everything. He waited for Waylon to speak.

"I thought about getting you flowers, but I didn't think you'd care about that. But I remembered you like these salty caramel candies." He held up the bag in his hand. "I had to get them delivered from two towns over since I couldn't find them here and I can't leave."

Audor bit the inside of his cheek. He would bet good money Waylon had never done anything like this for anyone. "I don't have anything against flowers. But I prefer the ones picked. Those come from the heart. Obviously, it's a bad time of year for that." Audor didn't know why he rambled.

Waylon shifted from foot to foot when Audor didn't invite him in. "I'm sorry. I'm not very good with words. The last thing I want to do is say something stupid and have you disappear before I can explain again. I don't usually talk this much."

He was adorable. Asshole. "You could've stopped at you're sorry."

Waylon nodded. "Okay. I'm sorry. Seriously. Before I well and truly ruined everything, I was trying—badly—to say I was happy I found you. You've made my life feel good." He swiped his hand over his eyes and Audor bit back a smile. "I don't know what words to use."

"It's okay. I can hear your thoughts."

Waylon shifted from foot to foot again. "Oh. Okay." He held out the bag to Audor. "I'll leave you alone."

Audor didn't take the gift. He snagged Waylon's shirt instead, slowly reeling him closer. "What if I don't want to be left alone?"

The hope in Waylon's eyes nearly broke Audor. Waylon was this huge alpha, but if anyone bothered to look, they'd see how vulnerable he was. He was sad and lonely. No one checked on him because he was the strong one. Sometimes Waylon was scarily close to giving up.

"I can't read your thoughts the way you can mine."

That confession sounded like it hurt Waylon's chest. As an ancient vampire, very few people could see inside his head. As his mate, it was Waylon's right and Audor was denying him. "Only one of us can remedy that."

He watched something solidify inside Waylon. His determination became like a physical thing. The space between them disappeared. Waylon kept moving, forcing Audor inside. He kicked the door closed behind him. The alpha had come out to play. As soon as they were closed away from the world, Waylon's mouth covered Audor's. There was no denying him. It felt like Waylon was everywhere. This was his mate. Possessiveness roared to life inside Audor. He couldn't tell any longer if it was his or Waylon's. It didn't matter. The bag of candy dropped. His feet left the floor as Waylon lifted him, holding two handfuls of ass. He marched toward Audor's bedroom, kissing a path down Audor's neck. His fangs brushed Audor's skin, making goosebumps cover his body.

Audor's back hit the bed.

Waylon's claws ripped through Audor's clothes. The knowledge he made Waylon lose control enough to be incapable of completely fighting off the change was empowering. Audor saw every inch of Waylon's mind. Not only had Waylon never lost control with anyone the way he always did with Audor, he also loved Audor. He had for a long time. That was the real problem. Waylon had been terrified of what would happen to his heart when Audor found his true mate. He hadn't thought he would survive it. Waylon just never knew how to say things like that. He felt like saying things aloud made them real. Maybe he would have set something in motion, ensuring Audor found a mate that would never be him. But it was him, and Audor wouldn't let him hurt ever again.

Audor flipped, rolling Waylon beneath him. Waylon was bigger and Audor should let him keep the illusion of being stronger. Right now, he needed everything. He sat back on his heels and then dove for the lube on his bedside table. Waylon fought to get out of his clothes. Audor snagged the material and easily tore it away—like his shirt and pants were made of cheap paper. He kissed Waylon's chest as he played with his own asshole, getting himself ready for the rough way Waylon would fuck him. Audor made his way down Waylon's body to his weeping cock. He felt everything Waylon did. Audor needed to know what would happen when he put Waylon's dick in his mouth. A loud moan escaped him at first suck. That was as much as he got before Audor ended up on his back, legs in the air, and Waylon's dick tearing him in two. Audor dug his fingers into Waylon's back, leaving bruises that would disappear as quickly as they appeared. He moaned as

Waylon rocked inside him, making Audor soar. Audor wanted to beg Waylon to bite him. He needed Waylon to feel everything the way he did.

Waylon's tongue swiped his neck, savoring the same spot over and over again.

"Please? Damn, baby. Please?"

Waylon struck. Air disappeared. It ceased to exist. All the mattered was the way his body danced with ecstasy. He tried to scream, but no sound emerged. Audor felt the second their souls became one. It was the most mind blowing and beautiful moment of his life. He wished he could do it a million times.

In the desperate throes of his orgasm mixed with Waylon's, Audor missed the way Waylon had gone completely still.

His face stayed pressed against Audor's chest. He smelled Waylon's tears. Audor snagged Waylon's chin and yanked, forcing Waylon to look at him. He was surprised he didn't accidentally rip off Waylon's head in his shock. Waylon's eyes were red. He looked completely lost and broken. "Why didn't you tell me you love me?" A stuttered and ragged-sounding breath escaped Waylon. "I would've given anything for those words."

Goddess. He truly did love this dumb wolf. "No. You would've decided you know what's best for me and never spoken to me again. You would've disappeared inside your head and convinced yourself cutting ties would be what's best. It was better to have some of you than none." Audor swallowed the anger and hurt that wanted to rise to the surface. He swallowed again when a lump rose in his throat. "So I saved you from me. Every second was like being set on fire, but I couldn't be how you wasted time any longer."

Waylon kissed his chest. "Can you still not see the lie in those words?"

"I'm sorry for disappearing. You deserved better from me. Odin came to see me."

Waylon's chin shot up. "What?"

Audor pulled the memory to the forefront of his brain so he could share it with Waylon. He felt Waylon playing in his mind. It was nice. He had been alone for a long time. While he could hear lesser beings' thoughts, that hadn't made him any less alone. This was different. Waylon was there, completely sharing life with Audor.

"You're a vampire of worth."

Audor blinked. He had gotten lost in his head. "What?"

Waylon's heart was in his eyes. "Odin said I was a wolf of worth and he wouldn't have chosen you. You're a vampire of worth. I would choose you in every life." He didn't give Audor time to get emotional. "You didn't feed enough the other night. I can feel your hunger. You were just angry and proving a point. You didn't actually take the blood you need."

That was all true. Truthfully, Audor had been closer to tearing Waylon's throat out than he was feeding.

"I would've preferred that if you didn't plan to come back."

Audor urged Waylon higher. "Staying away from you has never felt like a real option. Every second was hell." He nuzzled Waylon's neck.

Waylon took a shaky breath.

Audor went hard like he hadn't just blown. He scraped his fangs across Waylon's pulse point, dragging out the anticipation he felt growing inside Waylon.

Waylon shifted positions and grabbed their erections before holding them together.

Audor knew it was pointless to stroke. They were too connected in mind. Biting was too personal. Too erotic. The instant he sank his fangs into Waylon's neck, an orgasm tore through Waylon, pulling another from Audor. They were one mind, sharing the ecstasy of Audor's bite. Audor sucked. Waylon's body jerked in his hold. Audor took what he needed before retracting his fangs and licking the wound closed.

"Fuck, I wish—" The words died on Waylon's lips as he pulled away. His gaze locked on Audor's neck in disbelief, as if seeing it for the first time.

"What?"

Waylon's gaze moved to hold his stare. A smile exploded across his face. "Come on. I need to care for you anyhow." He rolled and climbed from the bed before pulling Audor along. Inside the bathroom, he started the shower. When he turned back Audor's way, he still wore a huge grin.

"What?" Even Audor heard the laughter in his voice. Waylon's brain was sunshine and rainbows, but Audor couldn't see what caused the sudden elation.

Waylon turned Audor toward the mirror. His arms wrapped around Audor from behind and pressed against his back. Audor's gaze automatically went to Waylon's reflection over his right shoulder, except that was not where his gaze landed. He stopped breathing. Everything stopped.

"I started to say I wish I could mark you for the world to see. It seems Celeste has me covered."

Vampires didn't scar. Yet there was Waylon's mark. He had been marked as Waylon's mate. Audor couldn't even blink. Never would he have expected to find a scar beautiful, much less one to match the level of gorgeousness as the mark he had left on his mate. But this was beyond beautiful. It was a miracle. They kept getting handed those and Audor knew he wasn't worthy.

Everyone will know you're mine.

Audor's throat swelled. They really would. He never dreamed he would have so much.

Chapter Six

THE SENSATION OF COLD and warm touching his spine slowly dragged Waylon from his dreams. He chuckled as Audor nipped at his skin, as if trying to tickle him. Audor marched cold pieces up his back, as if walking toy soldiers. Waylon couldn't stop smiling. He had never known this much happiness. Then Audor's hands appeared in front of his face as he draped himself over Waylon's body. Waylon gasped at the items Audor held.

"My beauty deserves pretty things. I found these too many years ago to count. All this time, I haven't known what I saved them for. Now I do. They're the rocks I wanted for my mate."

Waylon's hands shook as he took the stones. They were more than rocks. Waylon could smell them. The scent of nature lived in his blood. They were gemstones. Like genuine gems mined from stone. "Holy shit. These are likely priceless."

Audor kissed his shoulder. "No. You're priceless. I'm sure these have a dollar amount that could be assigned to them."

"Not to me. They're a gift from my mate." Part of Waylon wanted to say he could never accept such a huge gift, especially one given so casually, but they

126

were mated. Everything that was Waylon's was Audor's.

"And everything that is mine, is yours," Audor said, finishing his thoughts. "Speaking of which. We need to decide where we'll live. Your place is more con-venient for your work. I just bought this place and have been fixing up the garage. But that doesn't matter as much to me as you do if you'd rather stay where—"

The earth shook, cutting off Audor's words. He scrambled to ensure every inch of Waylon was covered from any danger. The moment passed as quickly as it happened, but all Audor's alarm bells were clanging. He leapt from the bed almost as quickly as Waylon. In a flash, Audor wore jeans and had a battle ax in each hand. "I must go to Frost. He's my duty."

Waylon pressed a quick kiss to Audor's lips and turned wolf. *My pack needs me. Don't close your mind to me.*

Audor gave him a sharp nod. "I love you, wolf." He dissipated, landing on Frost's front lawn at the same time as every guard assigned to Frost. They each held various weapons. Thankfully, dawn hadn't quite broken. He had woken Waylon early, hoping to steal some time with him before Waylon went to work. His powers weren't cut by the sun yet. They would be soon and Audor had no idea what danger they faced. Something unnatural had happened, though. It was a chill down his spine. Gemini was full leopard as he burst from the door. *What's happened?* Gemini's thoughts were as loud as a shout.

Audor ran for the door. "I don't know yet, but it's best we form a tight circle around Frost until we receive word things are clear." They poured inside.

Frost stood in the middle of the living room, wearing nothing but pajama pants. He held a cup of coffee and looked too exhausted to care if the apocalypse had just begun.

"You know earthquakes are common in this area, right?"

Leif closed the door.

Fen began checking windows. "Earthquakes don't feel like that. That's what it feels like when a demon horde breaks the veil."

Goddamn it. Audor knew the cold sensation down his spine felt familiar. It had been a long time since he felt this way. His gaze met Leif's. They had been raised together. They had been best friends since they were old enough to hunt together. Leif had also been at his side during the demon wars. They had seen what demons would do to this town.

It's a demon breach. Please be careful.

He felt the phantom sensation of Waylon caressing his mind, as if comforting him. *I'm checking the town now. If I get the faintest scent of evil, you'll be the first to know.*

"My mate is checking the town. He'll let us know what he finds."

"Mate? It had better be Waylon, or I'll flip this table."

Audor flashed Frost a smile at the words. He was so damnably calm, it was catching. Plus, Waylon's name had been mentioned. That was all Audor ever needed.

"Vampires and Weres can't be mates," Fen said, staring out the back door. His gaze kept moving in every direction.

Leif's eyes were locked on Audor's neck.

Audor stood at Gemini's side, keeping himself bodily between Frost and the door. "This vampire was blessed with a Were mate."

All eyes turned his way, as if that news trumped all danger.

Leif was the first to turn away. "Now isn't the time."

A shot of pain hit Audor in the chest. Until that moment, he had forgotten Leif had once been madly in love with a bear. The guy had been huge and cuddly. Funny and protective. It had ended badly for all the same reasons he had almost lost Waylon. Until that moment, he hadn't realized how much of that Leif still carried with him. There was no denying his friend's pain. It sat on his chest.

What's happening? I can feel your hurt.

Audor smiled. His mind was no longer his alone. *I'm fine, gorgeous. How are things going on your end?*

There's nothing. Randall and I have found a few lingering scents of sulfur, but nothing. If demons broke the veil, they didn't stay here. I'll keep checking until I've seen every pack member.

Be careful. They can possess people. Check everyone's scent.

I've got your back.

Audor smiled. He knew he did. "Waylon says he's found a few lingering scents of sulfur, but nothing more. It's as if any demon that broke the veil vanished as quickly as it appeared."

"Fuck." Fen's curse summed things up nicely. "They could be possessing any-one. The sun is rising, and demons aren't trapped by any such nonsense. We'll be sitting ducks soon."

A pair of demons appeared from Frost and Gemini's bedroom, as if they lived there. Thankfully, they were the good ones. Lire and Kallous were on Jonathan's team.

Gemini plopped down at Frost's feet, as if he knew he could relax now, but he didn't give up a defensive post of his mate.

Frost sighed. "We have to come up with some kind of system. People just stepping through mirrors as they please is becoming an issue."

Lire flashed a smile Frost's way. "It's no wonder Jonathan likes you." He focused on Audor. His eyes were ever changing, as if they couldn't pick a color. "We've come to help your mate. We can move freely in the sun and we can spot demon entrances better than anyone here."

Audor nodded. "Thank you. It's killing me to stay here, but this is my place."

Lire dipped his chin. "I understand. No harm will come to your wolf."

Leif stared out the front door.

Fen stared out the back.

Both men ignored everyone while anger practically vibrated from them.

Audor pinched a spot between his eyes. *Lire and Kallous are here to help.*

More hands make less work.

Audor smiled. The air lightened. His mate was fine. They had help. Everything would be okay.

Waylon was fucking exhausted by the time darkness fell again and the entire town had been searched. He let the hot water pour down from his shower, washing away the dirt of the run. He felt Audor coming. Waylon closed his eyes and turned his chin up, letting the water hit his face.

"Damn. That's sexy. Do you need someone to wash your back?"

Waylon hid a smile. He turned, ensuring Audor saw the erection he sported just from the thought of Audor showering with him. "You could do that, or you could start packing bags so we can go home."

He saw the way Audor fought hope. "You're willing to live with me?"

Waylon got it. Audor had just bought his house and wanted to make it a home. Waylon wasn't attached to his place. He was an animal. There had been many years he had lived in the woods. If Audor wanted to be the one who gave Waylon a real home, Waylon could live with that. His mate's happiness meant more to him than an extra few minutes' drive to work. "You're my other half. Of course, I want to live with you. You love your house, and I love you. That's all that matters."

Audor stepped inside the shower fully dressed. "I think I have time to get you off, pack your bags, and have you in bed in time to get your full eight before work tomorrow."

Waylon smiled so hard, his face hurt. He dragged Audor against him and took the kiss he was dying to have. Audor's hands were everywhere.

I'm so in love with you.

The words brushed Waylon's brain in the most loving of touches. His eyes burned and his throat swelled. Audor was a miracle so huge, Waylon had never dared to dream so big.

Waylon killed the shower. "Take me home."

With a single thought, Audor pulled Waylon through space and into the home they would now share.

Waylon stripped the soaked clothes from Audor. "You know I love you more than anything, right?"

"Yes." The breathless whisper from Audor was barely audible as Waylon kissed his way down Audor's neck.

"Try harder."

At his demand, Audor spoke louder. "Yes."

"Good." He spun Audor and shoved. Waylon bent Audor over and face down on the bed. "This is going to feel a lot like hate fucking."

Audor moaned and squirmed like he couldn't wait. "Yes. I want that."

Waylon knew he did. Audor liked it rough. Since Waylon was an alpha used to dominating, Audor was perfect for him. Waylon used the bare minimum of lube before he pushed his way inside Audor. He didn't go easy. He thrust hard, lifting Audor's feet off the floor from the power of it.

Audor clutched the blankets. "More."

Waylon had everything he needed. He eased out a hair and thrust again, doing his damnedest to make Audor feel as amazing as possible. Their shared pleasure was unlike anything he had ever known. He wasn't used to feeling everything Audor did mixed with his own desire. It was overwhelming. He didn't know if he would ever get used to it, but—for now—he couldn't focus on anything else. That meant holding the wolf back was nearly impossible. Parts of his body shifted without his permission. He kept trying to stop it. Waylon's claws accidentally cut through Audor's skin. A deep moan vibrated from Audor as the wounds healed. Fuck. He was just flawless in every way. Too perfect. Waylon didn't know how to make sex last when he couldn't even control his claws.

Audor suddenly scratched at the blankets and tried scrambling away. "Oh, fuck. Oh my goddess. What are you doing to me?"

Waylon panicked and dove into Audor's thoughts, trying to find out what he had done wrong. All he found was ecstasy.

Audor's pleasure damn near bordered on pain. He didn't know if he should pull away from it or lean into it. Waylon made the choice for him. He fucked him harder.

"Holy shit. What the hell?" More scratching and trying to crawl away. "You're—Jesus. It's—goddamn." A loud cry tore from Audor.

Waylon couldn't see or hear. The orgasm Audor had robbed him of his senses. It had Waylon humping the waves and babbling while pumping Audor full of cum. He fucking throbbed and Waylon hated when people used that description, but he got it now. Sex with his mate was mind blowing. He was afraid of how addicted he could become. Waylon wanted to chain Audor to the bed and fuck him until they both died. Then he tried to pull out so he could nuzzle his baby, and he couldn't.

Audor moaned.

A nervous laugh escaped Waylon as he realized why Audor had been trying to get away from him. "Oh no."

"Fuck. Please stop moving. You're still hitting at just the right angle, and I can't."

"I'm stuck."

Audor went completely still. Waylon heard him take a breath and hold it. He felt Audor in his mind, finding out for himself what Waylon meant. A loud laugh burst from Audor. He shook with it, making things worse.

"Damn, Audor. If you don't stop, we'll be here all night."

Audor wiggled his ass, making Waylon gasp as tiny aftershocks crawled up his dick, which had shifted.

"You know, I've been alive hundreds of years, and this is the first time I've knotted. I hope this is a new thing you plan to continue."

Waylon's embarrassment fled. A possessive growl vibrated in his throat. It was full wolf. *Mine.* He was on the verge of a complete shift. Audor's total acceptance of him had truly brought out the alpha. He wanted to lick and nuzzle. Waylon needed to prove he was worthy.

"Oh, gorgeous. You're more than worthy. You're every fucking thing to me."

Waylon dick finally slipped from Audor's ass. He wasted no time pushing Audor all the way into bed so he could join him to cuddle. He curled his large frame around Audor and licked—like a mother grooming her babies. If Audor thought it was weird, he didn't complain. Waylon purposely didn't listen to his thoughts. He didn't want his feelings hurt if Audor didn't really want this much of the wolf.

A happy hum caressed his ears. Audor scratched his head. "Damn. That feels good. Don't stop."

Waylon sneaked a peek at Audor's thoughts, trying to see if he only humored him. All he saw was happiness and love. Audor saw the moment exactly as Waylon intended: as an act of love, and he wanted it. Waylon nuzzled Audor's neck and kept his face hidden. He didn't want Audor to see the tears that filled his eyes. Audor was the miracle he shouldn't have gotten. He couldn't be more humbled and thankful. Odin had a slave for life.

Chapter Seven

As MUCH AS AUDOR hated leaving a sexy wolf in his bed, especially without waking him, Audor had to check on Frost while it was still dark. He made Waylon coffee and left a note, letting him know where he had gone. While Audor knew Waylon could simply ask him mentally where he was, he didn't want even a second of worry to touch his mate.

When he landed in Frost's front yard, he spotted Fen and Stone guarding the house. Thankfully, some months back, Riku had drawn protection spells around the house, making it impossible for any creature to get in without prior permission. It seemed King Jonathan's bunch were immune to that, but they were keeping Frost safe.

Fen headed in the opposite direction as soon as he saw Audor. Audor bit back a tired sigh. It seemed he had made an enemy out of that one. His gaze slid Stone's way. No animosity shot his way, so Audor assumed Stone understood Waylon was his mate. There was no sense in being angry. Waylon belonged to him and Audor belonged to Waylon. That was just the way of it. Still, Audor had red-hot coals of jealousy in his gut when he looked at Stone. He still saw the ballsy vamp on his mate's lap. His eye twitched. It was best he dealt with the hatred directed at him.

Audor searched out Fen. He appeared in his path before Fen could escape him. "Anything new to report?"

"It's been quiet." Fen moved to step around him.

Audor stepped into his path. "I owe you an apology."

"Then say it and move along." His bright green eyes sparkled with hatred. Audor knew things had gone south on their date, but he wasn't sure he warranted all this. Maybe it was the red hair. Gingers were said to be fiery.

"I'm sorry for how things went down at Frost's party. You didn't deserve that. At the time, I had no idea Waylon was my mate."

"You were aware you loved them, though."

It wasn't a question. Audor wouldn't pretend Fen was wrong. "Yeah. I knew. We had split, and I tried to move on. I never meant to hurt you."

A bitter laugh fell from Fen's lips. "This isn't hurt. I'm pissed. As you said, you knew how you felt. You also knew how Waylon felt. He's a lesser being. No doubt you read his every thought. You knew how everyone felt, and yet you willingly chose to drag me into things. I don't like being used."

"I do. Use me, daddy," Stone said, walking past them on patrol. The obnoxious baby voice he used had Audor pinching the spot between his eyes. Plus, he just needed a moment. As much as Audor chafed at Waylon being called lesser, he could only fight one battle at a time. He opened his mouth, unsure of what to say. All he knew was they had to work together to keep Frost safe and hard feelings could put them at risk.

A wildflower appeared between them. "Peace?" Waylon had to have been really hunting to find a flower this early into spring.

Fen's gaze dropped to the flower pointed his way.

Audor fought like hell not to look at Waylon. His eyes itched to see his mate. *You meant that flower for me.*

He practically felt Waylon's inner laughter. *I totally picked it for you, but this has to end. I'll pick you another.*

Fen didn't take the flower, but the rage left his eyes. "You picked that for your mate."

Waylon didn't give up trying to hand it to Fen. "It's still for my mate. If you two can't get along, then you can't watch each other's backs. I know you're both warriors who don't think you'd let something personal cloud your judgment in battle, but I won't risk it. Let's put this behind us. Let me make amends." He held the flower closer.

Fen finally took it. He eyed it for a second. "As you said, I'm a warrior. I'd never allow harm to come to anyone for personal reasons. Thank you for the flower. No one has ever given me one." On that note, he walked away, leaving Audor feeling worse than before. He had a bad feeling Fen had been happier about that date than he realized and obviously felt neglected because everyone saw him as a warrior and nothing else. Guilt ate at him. Then his gaze met Waylon's, and everything fell away except his other half.

"Hey."

Waylon smiled. "Hey. I woke up alone."

Now he felt twice as guilty. "I had to come to check on things before sunrise. But I made you coffee."

Waylon crowded his space. "You did and I appreciate it. But I want my morning kiss before work even more."

"Hmmm. Well, we can't have you going off to serve and protect without a kiss."

Waylon shook his head. "We really can't."

Audor wrapped his arms around Waylon and shuffled closer. His lips skimmed Waylon's. "How did you get here so fast?"

"Leif brought me."

"Good. That means I can do this." Audor zapped them home. Waylon was already in uniform. Audor couldn't seduce him the way he wanted, but he could ensure Waylon thought about him all day.

"I always do that no matter what."

Fuck. He loved having Waylon in his head. As much as he hated it, Audor swept one last kiss across Waylon's lips. "Be careful out there."

"Always. Get some sleep."

"I will." Audor knew, as much as he'd prefer to sleep when Waylon did, he needed his energy for when the sun went down. "If you need me, I'm still just one thought away."

"Same. I love you."

The sincerity in Waylon's eyes made his throat swell. This was everything he had ever wanted, and he wasn't sure if he was worthy. He would savor this blessing nonetheless.

Lucifer stared at the horizon. From the top of the mountain, he could see the whole town. He knew this was the real reason Riku chose this spot to live. This was Riku's charge. He was their sentry, while most people didn't even know he existed. Maybe that gave him purpose. Lucifer hated it. He wanted Riku with him. That was his place, ruling at Lucifer's side.

Warm lips pressed against the spot between his wings. Lucifer made them disappear so Riku could hold him tighter.

Riku didn't let him down. His arms tightened around Lucifer's waist. He gently stroked Lucifer's stomach. "Why do you tease this town?"

A bark of laughter burst from Lucifer. He wouldn't play dumb. They both knew he was the reason they scrambled, searching for demons. "I'm bored. These people could do with a little excitement."

"So you didn't do it to hurt me?"

Lucifer rolled his eyes, but he covered Riku's arms with his and linked his fingers through Riku's. "Did it hurt you?"

"No." The word brushed his skin with Riku speaking against his back between kisses.

"Then that was a ridiculous question." He tightened his hold on Riku, in case the words made him run away… again.

Riku pressed his cheek against Lucifer's back. "Don't listen to my thoughts for a minute."

"Okay." It was a lie. Lucifer didn't have the willpower to shut Riku out. If he could, this bullshit half–life would have ended long ago.

I love you. Fuck, I love you so much. This is killing me, and I don't know what to do. I can't destroy everything for my gain, but I'm slowly dying.

Lucifer stared at nothing and tried to breathe. He couldn't give away that he listened. Neither could Lucifer keep doing this. He had shown more patience with Riku and selflessness than he ever had since the beginning of time. This had to stop—for both their sakes. Then he felt it. A tear ran down his back. He was done.

"You have a week."

Riku sniffed. "What?"

Lucifer didn't turn. He couldn't look at Riku, or maybe he would cave. "You have a week to decide, or I'm choosing for you."

"What do you plan to choose if I don't?"

So much pain sat on his chest. His sister had found a new way to torture him. He had honestly believed there was nothing left she could do to him. Riku was the worst pain he had ever endured, and he had been ripped to pieces over and over for centuries.

"I don't know," Lucifer answered honestly. "Maybe I'll return to hell where emotions are cranked up to a million. You'll feel the loss of me in a way your mind likely can't endure." That was the thing about Hell. It found the tiniest seeds of longing and turned them into a nonstop torment that would break the strongest of minds. Unlike heaven, where emotions were muted to stop any pain, Hell was the opposite in every way. "Maybe I'll just take you and leave you no choice but the nightmare of being my mate. Or I could kill you and set myself free. I guess we both have a week to figure it out."

Riku didn't stop kissing his spine. It was like he couldn't stop, even when he fully understood Lucifer could break him in ways he didn't even understand. His brain couldn't wrap itself around the horror Lucifer could place upon him. Riku's imagination wasn't that big. Still, if Riku couldn't choose him, Lucifer would do what he had to do to end this. He was no one's toy.

"One week, Riku." With the promise hanging between them, Lucifer disappeared, escaping Riku's grasp. He couldn't stand being held anymore, knowing it was temporary and pointless. The world had seven days. Everyone needed to pray Riku chose him. Otherwise, he would level this place.

The day had been oddly quiet, considering yesterday's drama. At the end of his shift, Waylon pulled into the local market and headed inside. There was no food at Audor's place. As an ancient, he had lost interest in food a long time ago. Unlike Waylon, he didn't need food to survive. That thought led to another as he grabbed a basket and headed down the first aisle. In Were pairings, each life was tied to the other. Even though Waylon was damn near impossible to kill, it could happen. If he had a Were or human mate, they would likely join him in death so they could be reborn and find each other in the next life. Either the years would catch up or the separation would be too much to endure. One wouldn't last without the other. With Audor, he didn't know what would happen if anything happened to either of them. It was a terrifying thought. Over the years, he had met vampires who had lost their mates. It was ugly. The loss was unbearable, but they endured. Waylon didn't want that for Audor. He supposed that meant he could never die.

Waylon nodded as he passed a Were couple. They nodded back and then coldly looked away. It struck Waylon as odd, but everyone had those days. It was possible the couple were fighting or something else completely unrelated to him. By the time he passed the third person who blatantly cut him, a bad feeling overcame him. Then he spotted Ashka with Ashlee in her arms, booking it in his direction. His heart sank. He just wanted to go home to Audor.

Ashka grabbed his arm and pulled him aside, as if getting out of earshot, even though they were the only people in the aisle. "We have a problem. One of the new guys in town is going around telling everyone you're mated to a vampire."

"I am."

Ashka made an impatient gesture. "Yeah, I know. I don't care about that. Listen, he's getting people riled up, saying how unnatural it is and that you're tainting our pure bloodline. Obviously, that's ridiculous. It's not like you can have kids with another man or it would matter if you could. Anyhow, he's getting attention. He wants to challenge you for alpha." Ashka finished by chewing her lip. She was obviously upset on his behalf. He adored her for it. Waylon was also tired.

He sighed. "All right. I'll take care of it. Do you know where I can find this guy?"

"He was at the diner when I overheard his bullshit. I raced straight here, so I imagine he's still there. Big guy. Red wolf."

Waylon nodded. He knew who she meant. There was only one recent transplant that fit the description. "A pup. Fantastic." He glanced down at his groceries and sighed again. "Thank you for letting me know."

"Of course." She sounded exactly like it was a given. "You're our alpha. We don't know this guy. He could do anything to this town. Its people. You've always taken care of us. Just let me know if you need anything. Randall and I will be there."

Waylon nodded. This was not how he wanted to spend his night. "Thank you. Get home. Crazy ladder–climbing wolves are capable of anything."

Ashka nodded and headed for the door.

Waylon followed at a slower pace. If Waylon couldn't defuse this, he didn't want anyone to retaliate against Ashka for warning him. He had to pull the plug on this bullshit now before it became a full uprising. Waylon understood by waiting so long to introduce his mate, he had opened himself up to questioning whispers. If they had nothing to fear, why wouldn't he share his joy? He totally got it. This was a peaceful town and had been since day one. He would be damned if some random wolf sauntered into town and ruined what they had going just because Waylon had experienced a few days of personal drama. If a genuine challenger ever wanted to take his place, it would be one thing. But this one was obviously a scheming troublemaker. That didn't make for good lead-ership.

It took less than five minutes to get to the diner. The minute he walked through the door, the place fell silent. All except the dumbass who hadn't noticed and still ran his mouth.

Waylon moved to stand over him. "Out-side. Now."

The guy went still. He turned. His whiskey–colored eyes landed on Way-lon's chest before his chin lifted and he met Waylon's stare.

Proving he was dumb, he stood. "With pleasure." He headed for the door.

Waylon followed, nodding at familiar faces as he passed. Unlike the store, no one seemed cold. Showing up to take care of things was enough to prove his worth, but Waylon had to completely put an end to this bullshit. He didn't want to hurt anyone. If he let this go, he already knew it would come to that.

"What's your name?" Waylon asked the moment they were outside alone. He already knew it. Waylon had to give permission to any wolf who wanted to stay in this town. Yuri's presence was a favor for a friend a pack over. Waylon needed to start a calm and rational conversation somewhere.

"Yuri." He sounded like an angry young one. Tiresome.

"Welcome to Wulfe. I'm sorry I haven't had time to introduce myself yet. I'm Waylon. The alpha around these parts.

People are saying it's a position you want."

"You disrespect our bloodline."

People began to pour from the diner to watch.

Waylon kept his cool in the face of youthful rage. "My mate was chosen by Celeste, the way all mates are chosen. He was visited by Odin to bless our pairing. If you wish to take issue with things, you should take it up with them. This town runs smoothly. For the most part, everyone gets along. I can't have you disrupting the peace. So, choose. Fall in line or pick a new pack."

He took a step closer. "I think I'll stay right here. What do you plan to do about it?"

Waylon sighed. He just wanted to go home. "Don't make me do this. I haven't had to put a pup in his place in a long time. Let's not break the streak."

"Pup?" His features shifted. He obviously had little control over his wolf.

"Yeah. Pup. If you can't hold your temper during a simple conversation, you're not fit to lead. Choose. This isn't a get-back-to-me-later situation. Right now, swear your fealty or I'll show you the edge of town."

"I kneel to no one." He shifted. His clothes ripped to shreds around him, hanging from his furry body in places. He paced, watching Waylon. Measuring him. More people poured from the diner. This was bad. They were in the middle of town. This could be exposing their people. It was dark, but not so much humans couldn't see if they passed. Vampires popped in, proving the king already knew there was an issue. While Jonathan didn't really rule Weres, he would not tolerate exposure and had the gods on his side on that one. Punishment would be handed down. This kid had no idea what he started.

You can kneel to me.

The fact that Waylon could hear him without trying already proved he wasn't an alpha.

"Odin hasn't chosen this for you. You have a lot of growing up to do if you want a role with this much responsibility. Being alpha isn't sitting in a diner all day running your mouth. It's caring about the people, especially caring enough not to expose them the way you are now. Do you have any idea what'll happen if this ends up on the news? If hunters start flooding in? Do you even give a fuck or are you scared someone might have a bigger dick than you? Grow the fuck up and think about someone other than yourself. Then you can come see me. Until then, you'll fucking kneel."

He felt the young one's rage building. Waylon knew he would strike soon. He was right. A half second before he lunged, Waylon stepped to the side, dodging him like he was nothing. The move blackened the wolf's thoughts even more, especially since Waylon refused to shift. Waylon easily bested him in human form. He wanted Waylon's blood. Yuri didn't understand Waylon could see his every move before he played it because he was the fucking alpha of this town.

Again, Yuri lunged with bared teeth, going for Waylon's throat.

Waylon planned to wait until the last second to step away. He needed to prove a point. Yuri could either stop humiliating himself or Waylon would do this all night until the shame ran him from town. Except, a half second before Waylon stepped aside, Audor appeared between them.

An angry roar tore through the air. He held the wolf by his throat, easily snatching him from midair. His feet were nowhere near the ground. He struggled, but it was useless. No air reached his brain, with Audor squeezing his throat. "You dare to attack what's mine?" The words were growled through terrifying fangs. Audor looked like a killer. He saw inside Yuri's head. Yuri watched his life flash before his eyes, and it ended here.

Audor pulled Yuri in, going nose to nose with him. "You don't touch my mate."

Waylon knew he had to step in before Audor actually killed the pup. He stroked a hand down Audor's spine. "It's okay. He's just a kid shooting for a position way out of his league."

He felt Audor waver, but he was enraged. Audor wanted to snap Yuri's neck. He had the right as Waylon's mate to take the pup's life over this attack. Audor squeezed tighter for a second before he tossed Yuri away.

Yuri skidded across the pavement before he was back on his feet. His body heaved for air, but he didn't try to attack again.

"Make your choice."

At Waylon's demand, Yuri turned his head right and left, taking in the number of witnesses to his effortless defeat. He took a step back. A wave of sadness washed over Waylon. Sometimes winning wasn't really winning. Yuri took another step back. Waylon felt the way his mind raced. He turned and ran away, darting into the woods that surrounded the town.

Waylon's shoulders fell. He looked Audor's way. Audor still practically vibrated with rage. Waylon could only handle one issue at a time. He faced the crowd of onlookers. Some had already gone back inside, as if they had known exactly how things would end.

Waylon motioned toward Audor. "This is my mate, Audor. He cares every bit as much about this pack as I do. Celeste and Odin chose him for me, and me for him. If anyone else has a problem with that, speak up."

No one said a word. One by one, they dropped to their knees, kneeling before their new alpha mate. He wanted to tell them to get up. This wasn't necessary, but it was what Audor was owed. Waylon wouldn't put up with disrespect. This wasn't a bigoted town. They wouldn't be starting tonight.

The wolf growled out his pride.

Audor looked his way at the sound. "That was hot."

Waylon flashed him a smile. *Later. I have to squash this.* He focused on the wolves at his feet. "It's okay, guys. You can stand. We've never been fancy like that around here, but we have always been a peaceful community. I plan to keep it that way."

With a few grumbles of approval, people flooded back inside.

Waylon focused on the vamps, waiting to see what needed to be done. "I really hoped to be home by now, but I guess we need to make sure there weren't any human witnesses."

Leif made a dismissive gesture. "We've got it. You two have dealt with enough drama tonight."

Audor linked fingers with him. "Come on, baby. Let's finish getting those groceries before the store closes."

A huge smile exploded across Waylon's face. "You were paying attention every second, weren't you?"

Audor's smile was unrepentant. "I was not-so-patiently waiting for you to get home. Your pack needed to see you're cool-headed and your mate is willing to kill for you. They needed to know you had a worthy mate."

Waylon had to admit Audor's timely appearance went far into solving things quickly. No one would likely challenge him again.

"I love you. The gods really knew what they were doing when they chose you for me."

Audor let out an obnoxious fake laugh. "I think you'll find the gods chose you for me."

Waylon couldn't stop smiling. He absolutely could not wait to spend the rest of his life just like this: heading to the grocery store with his other half, playfully arguing about nonsense. It sounded like the perfect life.

Chapter Eight

AUDOR WATCHED A BLACK wolf prowl the woods from his spot in the trees. He knew damn well Waylon had his scent and knew where he hid. Still, he played along. The light of the full moon shimmered across Waylon's gorgeous fur. Audor was incredibly in love with his mate. He had been since long before they had been given the blessing of each other. Waylon was huge and strong, but he was also patient and kind. The people adored him for the love he showed them. Despite Yuri's attempt to undermine him, in a single day, everyone had immediately been on team Audor. They had accepted Audor and treated him with the same respect and kindness they showed Waylon. Just as it had been for Frost, Audor's willingness to always take part in these full moon runs helped smooth the way into acceptance and make friends. From day one, Audor had done his best to integrate himself into the community. From the first full moon run, he had known this would always be his home. He had known Waylon was special.

Amber eyes turned up his way. *Do you plan to hide all night? I want my mate.*

With ease, Audor leapt from the branch where he sat and landed lightly on his feet at Waylon's side. He ran his fingers through Waylon's thick fur. "Do you have any idea how beautiful you are?"

Howls filled the air.

Waylon turned his head and sniffed the air, as if checking on his pack before giving Audor his attention again. He pressed his massive weight against Audor, nuzzling him. *You smell like my dreams come true.*

Waylon didn't need to explain. Scent meant a lot to wolves. As Waylon's mate, Audor's scent would be special and unique to Waylon.

Audor sat on a patch of thick grass and kissed Waylon's snout.

Waylon used his weight against Audor, knocking him onto his back.

Audor couldn't stop smiling as Waylon settled in close and draped half his body across Audor. He ran his fingers through Waylon's fur as he stared at the moon. The sounds of animals plowing through the woods and taunting their mates was like a strange sort of music.

I caught you.

A bark of laughter burst from Audor at Waylon's claim. "Yeah, you did, sexy hunter. You're a master of the chase."

Amber eyes turned his way. *Are you teasing me?*

"I would never."

Waylon shuffled higher until he was crushing Audor with his massive weight. He nosed at Audor's neck and licked.

A shaky breath escaped Audor. "Now who's the tease?"

A rustle came from the nearby brush. Waylon immediately went on defense. He crouched over Audor, staring at the tree line. A low growl vibrated from the back of his throat. A large red wolf eased his way out, crawling on his stomach and obviously showing he meant no harm.

Waylon turned human.

The red wolf did too. It was Yuri. He looked like hell. His eyes were red-rimmed. He looked much younger than Audor expected. In his rage, he had seemed older and more jaded. Audor realized now he was more likely the Were equivalent of a teenager.

"You okay?"

Audor forced himself not to smile. He knew the kid wouldn't appreciate the gesture and Audor wasn't laughing at him. He was just so damn proud of his mate. Every day, he proved why he deserved his position. He had a strength in kindness that was undervalued in their world.

Yuri looked defeated. He didn't meet anyone's gaze. "I'm sorry about yesterday."

Waylon's mind was a mess of sympathy and fatherly love. He hadn't wanted Yuri to run away to begin with. Dealing with youthful rage was a minefield. "I know what happened to your family. No doubt this is a hard transition for you."

What happened to his family?

His father was northeast alpha. The pack tore him and his mate to pieces before banishing Yuri. He's very young.

Waylon kept talking to Yuri, hiding their private conversation. "But this is a peaceful town. We want you here, but we also want to keep the amazing sense of community we've built."

The moment Waylon said he wanted Yuri, Yuri's gaze moved to hold Waylon's stare and didn't budge.

Waylon kept going. "I know you're not your father and you deserve the same respect, affection, and opportunity as every other Were in this town, but you have to give the same courtesy to everyone else. Do you think you can do that?"

What did his father do?

He claimed first rights with the chil-dren.

Audor flinched. That was an old rite that had died centuries ago. The alpha got the first shot at each Were in their pack before they mated with anyone else. It was supposedly about keeping the bloodline strong. Truthfully, it was just the sick mind of a sick leader.

Yuri swallowed. "Yes, sir."

Waylon kept his voice kind but firm. "Do you swear fealty to me and promise to do no harm?"

"Yes, sir."

Goddess, he sounded so young and vul-nerable.

Waylon gave him a sharp nod. "Okay. The pack will know, and they are the most accepting animals in the world. Go enjoy the run. It sounds like everyone is still having fun. I know they'll be happy to have you."

In an instant, Yuri was a wolf again. He was off like a rocket, leaving them alone.

Audor swiped his fingers through Waylon's hair. He couldn't be prouder of his other half. "You're a good man. I'm lucky to have you."

Sad eyes turned Audor's way. "I hope he doesn't make me regret it. And I'm the lucky one here." Waylon lowered his head and swiped his lips across Audor's. "Where were we?"

Leaves shook again, interrupting them.

Frost ran past them, laughing.

A snow leopard was playfully on his heels, very obviously holding back his speed.

Waylon chuckled and stole another kiss. "No one can say Frost doesn't fit in here."

"For several reasons," Audor agreed. He couldn't stop running his fingers through Waylon's soft hair. It felt exactly like his fur. Audor was unhealthily attached to touching him.

"I think it's inevitable we'll have an audience tonight unless you want to call it a night."

Audor might have been ashamed of how hot the idea made him if he didn't know

Waylon was the same. "Mhmm. An audience. A bit of exhibition? I'm in."

Waylon laughed just as Audor hoped. He claimed Audor's mouth, and the mood instantly changed. Things went from playful to serious in a flash. Waylon would be inside him soon, pulling all the cries and moans from him. This was the greatest life.

It hadn't been that many moons since Waylon thought he would never have this with Audor. He had loved him and lived in fear of that feeling. Now he had this perfect life, and he still lived in fear. If he lost Audor, he would lose himself.

"You can't lose me." Audor swiped his hand over the curve of Waylon's ass. "You're supposed to be focused on me right now instead of having these bleak thoughts." He squeezed Waylon's ass. "I demand my mate's attention."

Waylon felt how huge his smile had grown. He popped the button on Audor's jeans. "Attention, huh? Sounds like you need to be groomed."

Audor groaned.

Waylon saw in Audor's mind that he understood. Waylon intended to lick every inch of Audor until he begged for mercy. He pushed Audor's shirt up and started with his right nipple before tonguing his way to the left. The way Audor's breath stuttered made the wolf's pride grow. His mate was well taken care of. As he licked his way down Audor's stomach, he realized his mistake. He felt everything Audor did. Audor's desperation was his. Waylon had Audor's cock in his mouth way sooner than he planned. All thoughts of torture fled. He gave his everything. It was as if he sucked his own dick, which—as a wolf—he could do.

A groan escaped Audor. "Fuck, Waylon. You're killing me. The images in your head are hot as hell. I want to watch you bobbing on your own cock." He tugged Waylon's hair. His hips lifted. Audor abused his throat, and Waylon loved every second. The pressure climbed his erection as it did the same for Audor. The closer he got, the faster and harder he sucked. By the time he thought he might lose his mind, Waylon was ready to scream. Then the pounding pressure exploded into waves of bliss. He kept going until he licked away every drop. Then he kissed a path back up Audor's body.

"Goddamn. That was hot. Too quick for my liking, but it still got me hard."

At the sound of Stone's voice, Waylon buried his face against Audor's throat. He shook with laughter. Waylon had known Stone was there, just out of sight.

But Waylon had also felt Audor's satisfaction at knowing Stone watched. It was less about exhibitionism and voyeurism and more about Audor wanting Stone to fully see Waylon belonged to him. There would be no competition. Waylon was Audor's heart, body, mind, and soul. In fact, they shared the same soul now. They were unbreakable.

Keep an eye out for the next Devilish, *Undesirable.*

About the Author

CHARITY PARKERSON IS AN award-winning and multi-published author with several companies. Born with no filter from her brain to her mouth, she decided to take this odd quirk and insert it in her characters. One of her greatest loves is writing morally gray characters. You'll find them scattered throughout her hundreds of titles.

*Nine-time Readers' Favorite Award Winner

*2015 Passionate Plume Award Finalist

*2013 Reviewers' Choice Award Winner

*2012 ARRA Finalist for Favorite Paranormal Romance

*Five-time winner of The Mistress of the Darkpath

Connect with her online:

*Sign up for her newsletter: https://bit.ly/charityparkersonnewsletter

*Join her readers' group on Facebook: http://bit.ly/CharitysTribe

*Website: https://www.charityparkerson.com

*A list of her social media accounts and giveaways all in one place: http://hy.page/charityparkerson